The Halloween Promise

JEANNE ADAMS

DEDICATION

This book is dedicated to my family and friends - all those wonderful people who know writers are different and love us anyway.

And to the Spirit of Halloween, both fun and serious. For the joy of playing dress-up and scaring away the ghosties and goblins. For the turn of the seasons and for the celebration of the Harvest.

I'm tremendously grateful for the many gifts I've been given.

Happy Halloween!

CONTENTS

The Halloween Promise

JEANNE ADAMS

PROLOGUE

Boston, Massachusetts
October, The Year of Our Lord, 2016

"Goddamn dog," Turk cursed. Although the dog lay unconscious, maybe dead, Turk and his companion were bleeding from multiple bites. They'd incapacitated the dog, or so they thought. But even in his drugged state, the massive German Shepherd Dog had attacked.

Two of their companions finished in the back of the house and came out with their slight burden. With silent nods, they moved to the waiting SUV with it's blacked out windows gleaming in the security lights mounted on the house.

In the cloudy dark of the October night,

the sleek vehicle sped away with a little girl lying bound and unconscious on the back seat.

"Throw the damn dog in the back of the van, Mick." Turk growled, keeping his voice low as he wrapped his arm with gauze and tape. "Stupid drugs didn't work."

The other man grunted at the dog's weight. "Or he didn't eat all the meat."

Within minutes, they too had pulled away from the elegant home in Boston's Back Bay. The nanny and the housekeeper, tied and drugged in the spotless kitchen, had never seen any of them. The gas they'd used had put the women out within seconds.

"Let's go," Turk said, climbing into the driver's seat. "We're at time."

The op had been calculated down to the second. They'd built in ten minutes as a safety gap, but dealing with the fucking dog attack had eaten every minute of the margin.

It was a silent drive northward out of Boston's upscale neighborhoods, and through the northern suburbs. Taking a quieter rural road, they maneuvered through late night traffic in Salem, and out into the emptiness of rural Massachusetts. On the dark, deserted road between Pennyfield and the Merrimack River, they stopped to dump the dog. This far from Boston, no one would connect the body of a stray dog, dead in the road, with the missing girl's guard dog.

Mick snapped on a pair of rubber gloves then used his boot knife to neatly slice off the dog's collar. That, he tossed into the van. With a quick twist of his wrist, he cut off the end of the dog's tail. Then, with a grunt, he lifted the dead weight of the German Shepherd.

"Jesus, what the hell do they feed this dog, bricks?"

"Toldja he was heavy," Turk said, grinning from the driver's seat.

The patter of rain on the windshield was a welcome helper. In fact, the storm was absolutely perfect. People didn't look around when they drove in bad weather. The dog wouldn't be found until morning, if then.

Mick laid the dog on the slick, black macadam in the middle of the northbound lane and ran back to the van.

He saw Turk look in the rearview mirror and checked behind them. Headlights were a faint wink in the distance. In a few minutes the Shepherd would be history, and he wouldn't have to kill the dog.

He wasn't squeamish about people, but animals weren't on his hit list.

"You're brilliant, Mick," Turk complimented with laugh.

"Yeah. No blood in the van, no dog anywhere to be found. When the cars are through with him, all anyone will see is another flattened, road kill farm dog."

He dropped the bloody end of the dog's tail into a Ziplock, and that into a FedEx envelope. Dr. Thomas Spradling, III, would receive the bloody tail in the morning. The ransom note would come in another FedEx, along with a lock of his daughter's long blonde hair.

They were in the money now.

Adele rolled down the driver's side window to let in the October wind. She was exhausted, and she needed the rush of air to stay awake.

She was grateful that her sturdy truck was easy to drive even on the rain-slick road, because she was exhausted. She'd been helping another vet in a neighboring county with a foaling draft horse in distress. The big mare hadn't wanted the help, so Adele felt like she'd been playing football with the New England Patriots. Her back twinged, her arms felt like limp spaghetti and her legs and feet ached from standing so long.

She turned to get her bottle of water and fumbled for it in the dark. That was when she realized she had blood and hay stuck on her sleeve.

"Dammit, I changed my shirt." Somehow she'd managed to mess up the clean shirt too. That meant she'd have to wash two shirts, and her pants, and probably the door of the truck. Ugh.

She couldn't wait to get home to Haven Harbor. The vets up here in the upper, more rural, part of Massachusetts had a loose network amongst themselves. If any of them needed an extra hand, or coverage on a tough case, they supported one another. George Barrett had called her that afternoon, frantic that he might lose both the mare and the foal.

"That was actually yesterday, Adele," she said, talking to herself to try and stay awake. "Hell. Another night of short sleep." She and George had worked with the mare for almost nine hours, getting the foal turned. Adele, with her strong, but much narrower arms, had finally managed the feat, and the mare had effortlessly done the rest once that problem was solved. "Veterinary medicine," she intoned, laughing at herself. "Not for sissies." She grabbed her water bottle for a swig. The icy liquid helped keep her awake, but damn, bed was going to feel like heaven.

Off in the distance, she saw taillights, and wondered who else was out on the road this late. Her cell pinged with an incoming email. It popped up on the dashboard's display.

Dan Nutter. He was reminding everyone about a Coven leadership meeting on Tuesday and the Coven meeting on Thursday.

Heat uncurled in her gut. She wasn't sure what the hell she was going to do about her serious hankering for the quiet librarian. Gods, he was not only smart as hell, he was built like Adonis, straight out of a woman's Chippendales fantasy. They'd shared a kiss at the Midsummer BBQ and she'd nearly melted in lust. They'd sidled around one another ever since. So much had happened with the Witches Walk, though, they hadn't made a date.

She hoped he would ask, even as she questioned her attraction.

Why a librarian? What the hell was that about? Did she get the hots for a CEO or another small business owner? Oh no, not her. She got all googlie-eyed and hot and bothered over a director of libraries.

"Get a grip, girl. It's not like he's working at Seven-Eleven or something." He so didn't look like a book nerd, though. She knew he traveled regularly and he hung out with four of the most eligible bachelors in Haven Harbor. Make that three eligible guys—Mari Beecham had well and truly taken bachelor number one, Pere Hestworth, off the market.

Other than that, however, Dan, Dan the Librarian Man was a man of mystery.

She shifted in the seat, pumping the volume on her radio. "C'mon, girl. You can make it. Quit blinking those sleepy eyes," she remonstrated with herself. With only a few more minutes to go before she got to the bridge and Haven Harbor, she wasn't going to pull off the road for a nap. She wanted her own bed.

Adele rounded a curve and barely had time to slam the brakes on as her headlights picked out the still form in the road.

"Effin bloody hell!" she snarled as she fought the steering wheel. The tires squealed on the wet pavement and she shuddered to a stop, inches from the huge dog lying in the road.

In the glow of her headlamps she could see the dog was a big, healthy-looking German Shepherd. Cursing every unscrupulous dog owner in existence, she jumped out and ran to kneel by the unconscious animal. The male dog was still breathing. The respiration was shallow and slow, but it was still there. He was bleeding from somewhere, but in the darkness, she couldn't tell where. She ran her hands over him, not feeling anything torn or broken.

"Poor baby," she whispered, concentrating on the dog's life energy. It was sluggish but steady. Underneath that temporary weakness was a deep well of fierce strength.

The sound of a car coming from the north alerted her. It slowed as it approached, pulling up right by her. She raised a hand to screen the glare from the headlights as a tall, lean figure stepped out of the low-slung sports car.

"Adele?"

Speak of the devil, and he shall appear.

Relief and surprise flooded through her in equal measures, followed hard by heat. Dan Nutter's voice was pure sex, low and rich and deep.

"Hey," she managed to squeak out the word. "You've got the best timing."

"Yeah, I get that a lot. How can I help?"

Just as fast as the heat had come, a chill shivered over her. How did he always know where to be, and when to be there? She shrugged off the thought. She realized he would solve a huge problem.

"Help me get this big, beautiful guy into the truck. I have to get him to the clinic, and see if I can save him." She hadn't been sure she could lift the massive animal.

With an ease she envied, and with no concern for his clothes, Dan lifted the dog in his arms. She raced to open the crew-cab door on her truck and yanked out one of the blankets she kept in a bag behind the seat. She threw the soft cover over the leather and stepped out of the way.

"I'll follow you in," he said, opening the driver's door for her before turning back to his car. She was about to say he didn't have to, when she realized she'd have to get the dog out of the truck and into the clinic somehow.

She peeled out, racing for Haven Harbor with her fantasy guy hot on her tail.

The thought made her grin despite her worry for the gorgeous, wounded pup riding silently behind her.

"He followed me home, mom," she said, snorting out a laugh. "Can I keep him?"

Countless children, including Adele herself, had cheerfully used those same words to plead with their moms about rescuing strays. In this context, the stakes were much higher.

CHAPTER ONE

Wide awake now, Adele turned into the clinic parking lot. The security lights blinked on, letting her easily find the right key and get the door open. She punched in the security codes, shutting off the alarm.

"Bring him in here," she said, as Dan sidled in the door, trying not to bang any part of the wounded dog's body on the door. It was a challenge because the dog was large, even for a Shepherd. Dan followed her across the lobby and into the back room. She turned the lights on as she went, setting up a chorus of barks, whines and plaintive meows from the dogs and cats resting in kennels for boarding or recovery.

Adele spread a well-washed towel onto the shiny, stainless steel table, and helped Dan lay down his burden.

"Hang on a sec. I have to get out of this shirt." She ran to her office and tossed off the stained denim shirt, and the t-shirt under it. She tugged a clean Witches Walk Volunteer t-shirt from the bottom desk drawer, and over her head, then hurried back out. Dan was petting the dog and the sight of his tall, lean form was enough to get her heart rate jumping.

Slipping her hands into a pair of purple latex gloves, Adele began a minute examination of the dog under the bright lights.

"Poor pup." His pupils were dilated, and his color response slow when she pressed on his gums. "Crap, I'm going to need x-rays," she muttered, her hands moving carefully over the dog, looking for broken bones, evidence of swelling or punctures. She puzzled over the lack of any sign of an HBC, but sometimes, a glancing blow did damage without it showing. "If he was HBC, he might have internal injuries."

"HBC?"

"Hit by car."

"People suck," Dan growled, and she nearly jumped out of her skin. The low rumble was so unexpected and so close, that when she turned her head, he was right there just behind her.

"They do." Telling her hormones and her thundering pulse to behave, Adele turned back to her exam. There was a bloody gash on the dog's beautiful, broad head. "Here hold pressure on that while I finish checking him. Dammit, whoever dumped him did a number on his tail." It was still bleeding, but like the head wound, it was clotting. "This doesn't make sense," she murmured, running expert hands over the tail.

"What doesn't?"

"That isn't from being hit by a car." Adele gestured toward the dog's tail. "It's too precise a wound." She pressed gauze on the mangled tail. It had to be painful, but the dog didn't flinch. "I need to get an IV line started, and give him fluids. Then I'll stitch this and the head wound up before he comes around." She frowned over the dog's state. "He doesn't have a lot of injuries, nothing consistent with an HBC."

Dan nodded, and she caught herself staring at him.

"Anyway, let's wheel him into my x-ray station over there." She waved toward an area that could be curtained off. "And get that done, then I can shave and suture his head and tail."

She stroked a hand down the dog's side as they moved the table to x-ray. Her probing fingers hadn't found additional injuries or a collar, but the "dent" in the thick ruff of fur around his neck, and around his midsection, said he'd worn a substantial collar and possibly a harness, until very recently.

"He's in really good shape for a drop off," Dan said, and she realized he was petting the dog as well. When they stopped in x-ray, Dan returned to keeping pressure on the head wound.

"I really hate people who do that, drop off dogs on some country road because they're too much trouble , or whatever reason," she said, with some heat. "Let me see." She motioned for him to lift the gauze. The wound had stopped seeping blood. "Okay, that's good." She lifted her head to say something to him and, again, he was right there, his face inches from hers. She could feel his breath on her cheek.

"Why do you think he's a dropoff?" Dan asked, his hand rising to tuck a strand of hair behind her ear.

Panicking at the feelings he instilled in her, she jerked up. "We get a lot of it. Rural roads. An unwanted dog or cat just gets dumped." She shifted further away. "I need to get the x-rays. You don't have to stay if you'd rather go home."

Smooth, Adele, smooth. Throw him out, why don't you?

"I'll stay, and help if I can."

She nodded, not trusting herself to speak. "Okay. Great. Thanks." She pulled the machine over to the dog and set it up.

"Step out beyond the curtain," she ordered, as she went behind the screen and set the buttons on the console. It took only a few minutes to get the x-rays and set them to process.

"What now?" Dan asked, as they moved the dog back into the main room, under the lights.

Adele peeled off her gloves and pulled a suture pack. She rummaged in another drawer for the little machine that would read if the dog had an imbedded ID chip.

"What's that?"

"It'll let me check and see if he's microchipped." When Dan looked puzzled, she added, "an ID chip under the skin."

She paused and nearly shivered when his hands covered hers, taking the machine gently from her. "I'll see this through with you, Adele. Don't worry, I'm not squeamish."

She felt like an idiot, the way she was reacting to him.

Get a grip, doctor. Be a professional.

"Okay, um, here, put these on." Dan took the gloves she handed him, and, without being asked, tilted the light so it better shone on the dog's head.

"Thanks. You ever need a job as a vet-tech, you're hired."

He laughed and the velvety sound sent a frisson of delight through her bones. She got the shaver out of a basket on the counter, and shaved a patch on the dog's front leg, shaved around the head wound, and along the tail above the injury.

She hung a bag of Ringers to give the dog fluids, and slid the needle into the vein on the foreleg. Taping it in place, she moved onto the next thing.

With care, she brushed the shaved fur away from the cut, then disinfected it before bending low to peer at it. "This isn't as deep as I thought, but it still needs stitches. If you'll hold his head for me, again," she requested, tilting the dog's heavy, broad head into just the right angle.

Laying a sterile suture cloth over it, she made quick work of stitching up the wound. It was long, but shallow.

"So how does the microchip reader work?" Dan asked, breaking the silence. He had a deep restfulness to him, Adele decided. It was easy to be around him, even as he excited her senses.

"We'll scan to see if this big boy is chipped, call the company with the chip and they call the owners. The owners call us. Hopefully they actually registered the chip and paid the yearly fee so we can find them."

Dan continued to be helpful as she moved to the dog's tail and worked efficiently to clean, examine and treat the wound. The tail wound was far more complicated, but she set the last suture and cleared everything up. Dan had already turned on the little machine. "Where do I scan him?"

"Usually between the shoulder blades or low on the back of the neck."

The scanner immediately beeped with a number and information.

"HomeSafePets," Dan read, then detailed both the long registration number and the 800 number for the company. "I'll write it down."

"Idiots! Pay good money for a beautiful dog then leave it loose to get hit." She smoothed the coarse fur of the dog's ruff. "This is a purebred, for sure. And dogs like this don't come cheap."

"What next?" Dan stood, a quiet presence that still managed to set her nerves on fire, in the best possible way.

"I check the x-rays," she said, going to do just that. She came back in with the flimsy plastic rectangles. She snapped them into a lightbox and turned it on.

Dan moved to stand just behind her, but close enough to make her blood hum. Since her husband's death, she didn't often let men that close, but with Dan, it seemed natural. To her surprise, the desire to lean into his warmth was strong.

Pay attention, woman!

Frowning, she did focus on the x-rays. "This is weird. There's nothing. Not even a fracture under that head wound."

"Does that mean he was just dumped and not hit?"

She nodded, thinking. "Maybe. We'll see. I should probably do a tox screen, for poison."

"Toxicology? Why?"

She turned her head to look at him. "Just a hunch."

He smiled and her heart decided to gallop in her chest. Over a smile.

"That's good enough for me. What do we do?"

Adele showed him how to hold off the dog's vein on the leg opposite where she'd put in the line for fluids. When he'd done so, she drew blood for the screening. It would be expensive, so she'd hold off sending it until the dog's owner was contacted. They might not want to pay for it. But, if it was poison, it would be out of the dog's system within hours. If she was going to get good a sample, she had to do it now.

"Okay, that's good." She held pressure on the small spot where she'd drawn blood, then smiled at Dan. "You get to show your brawn again, good sir. Do you mind carrying him over to the kennel area? I'll bring the fluids if you'll carry the dog."

"Got it."

They settled the Shepherd in a large, mid-level kennel and covered him with a warming blanket. A meow had her shifting the portable table against the kennel wall. Ribald, the clinic cat, jumped onto the table to see the newcomer.

"Hey kit," Dan said, stroking a long-fingered hand down the cat's smooth black back. "Who's this?" he said to Adele as the cat purred and wound around Dan's hand. Dan continued to pet him.

"Ribald." When Dan laughed, she did too.

"No, I didn't name him," she said. "He was old Mrs. Perkins' cat. Her daughter's allergic, so we took him in when she passed away. He'd boarded here a lot when Mrs. P was traveling, so he knew us."

She folded several plush towels on the table and Ribald daintily stepped onto the towels and settled in to watch the dog.

Dan gave her an inquiring look.

"Ribald likes to sit with the recovering animals. He'd rather be up against the dog, but since I don't know the animal, I'm not going to chance that."

Dan nodded and once again ran a finger over her cheek, catching the brown-red tendril of loose hair and tucking it behind her ear. Again. "You're very skillful," he said, watching her with an intensity that made her want to squirm. "And you have a lot of compassion."

"Thank you." The moment was charged with an intense energy.

"You're welcome."

"You know I've been wanting to ask you out, right?"

"Yeah." Her voice was husky, and she couldn't help it, she rested a hand on his chest. "So why haven't you."

Dan had asked himself the same question. It came down to fear, really. He'd been out of the game for a while and his life never seemed to settle down. Since that didn't look like it would change, why had he waited?

"Will you go out with me Adele?" He watched her lips part and couldn't resist the invitation. Bending down, he brushed his lips across hers. The connection, hot and immediate, seared through him.

Adele moved in to him, her fingers gripping his shirt. Between deeper and deeper kisses, she said, "What are we doing?"

"Saving a dog," he managed to say as he easily picked her up to set her on the table they'd used to move the dog. "And you're deciding if you want to date me."

Ribald wasn't amused at their intrusion, but he didn't jump down either. To Dan's delight, Adele spread her legs, pulling him in close before sliding her hands into his hair. He felt the contact like lightning. She was smart, caring, and beautiful—an irresistible combination in his mind.

It had been just as hot before, when they'd kissed at the Midsummer BBQ, as the fireworks exploded above them. But she'd backed off, probably because he'd turned around and left for three weeks on a job for the FBI, his former employer.

Since then, they'd danced around one another at every Coven meeting and town event. He'd been dreaming about that kiss, waking up frustrated.

All this flashed through his mind as they continued to kiss, her breasts pressed into his chest with an amazing lush firmness that ramped up his desire.

"Adele," he murmured, between kisses. Dan wasn't sure if they'd have stopped with kisses, but the urgent beep-beep-beep of her phone broke them apart. "Do you need to get that?"

Adele nodded and rested her forehead on his chest for a moment as she caught her breath.

"Wow, you sure can kiss," she said with a smile as he helped her off the table. She made for her cell phone, checking the readout. She groaned.

"Oh, man, I need this like a hole in the head."

"What?"

"Emergency with the Lafayette's poodle, and her puppies. I told them to call me, day or night. The dog's got at least one really big puppy in there, if the sonogram's correct, and sometimes that big one has trouble coming out. It can put the whole litter in jeopardy."

"Do you need help?" Dan moved behind her and couldn't resist the urge to stroke a hand down her hair, tugging just a little on her ponytail. He was fascinated with her hair. It was a rich brown, streaked with red and a little gold. It was beautiful and silky under his hands.

She slanted him a look, "Thanks, but I don't think the mama dog would like too many new people around. She's pretty high strung."

"Okay. Are they coming here or are you going there?"

"I'll head out to them." She stretched up to kiss him, keeping it light. "Thanks though, for all your help."

"I'll walk you to the truck.

She shut down the lights and locked the doors as they stepped into the crisp October night.

"So now that you know I'm serious about that date," he began, and she laughed. "How about it?"

Damn, but he was a smooth operator.

She hesitated, just a moment, but then she gripped his arms, pulling him close on her own accord. He swooped in for another kiss.

It was as hot and fabulous as the amazing kisses they'd shared in the clinic.

What the hell was she supposed to do about that?

He broke off, pulling her in for a full body hug. There was no doubt about his interest. The hug made it obvious that, with Dan, everything was proportional. His height and stature were played out in the incredible feel of his arousal against her stomach.

Big gloves, big shoes, big…

The irreverent thought was cut off by another bing of a text from her cell.

"Crap, I have to go." She opened the truck and jumped up into the seat.

"Drive safely," he rumbled and shut her door for her. She rolled down the window as she started the engine.

"I will." He leaned in and kissed her again. She wanted to lap him up like chocolate. "Thanks for everything."

As she pulled out of the parking lot, she checked the rearview mirror. He was standing under the lights, watching her go.

####

Adele checked her watch as she stumbled into her kitchen, dropping her purse and emergency bag by the table. Five-thirty in the morning. Her dogs, Hercules and Patronus swirled around her, sniffing everything and woofing in greeting. She let them out into the fenced yard to do their business, and tried to make her fogged mind work.

She'd been exhausted before the incident with the injured dog. Now, after helping Mimi, the Lafayette's poodle, successfully birth nine healthy pups, including the one oversized male pup, she was beyond drained and well into useless.

She let the dogs in, as she tried to weigh if it was worth it to sleep until eight or if she should just shower, load up on caffeine and go in to work. When she swayed where she stood, she decided she'd be no good to anyone without a few hours to recharge.

"Sleep it is." Setting her alarm, she stumbled to her bedroom, kicked off her shoes and fell facedown onto the covers. The dogs jumped up and settled against her, and within seconds she was asleep.

She dreamed of Jeremy, and Mexico, and terror. Even as she dreamed a part of her wondered why this dream, and why now?

The dream haunted her even when she awoke.

"My therapist would have a field day," she muttered as she got out at the clinic. "New guy arrives in your life, you have to obsess over the one that hurt you. Yeah, yeah, yeah.

Screw you, subconscious," she said defiantly as she walked in and got ready for work.

After a full morning of appointments, most of which she'd had to push back because of an emergency, Adele was finally able to sit down and call the HomeSafePets eight hundred number. Time to locate the owners of her mystery patient. The dog was awake and alert, and seemed to be fine other than the head and tail wounds. That made her even more suspicious.

Adele was glad she'd taken blood for a potential tox screen, because all evidence pointed to him being drugged or poisoned, rather than hit.

Then again, if he'd been drugged, his wounds were even more suspicious…

The HomeSafePets clerk took her name and number and promised to track down the owners and put them in touch. Adele knew it might be hours before they contacted her, so she got back to work. As she pulled an old dog's abscessed tooth, she thought about Dan. Giving routine shots to a young pup, she was distracted by the memory of his incredible mouth, and incredible body.

Gods, that chest! Her hands had roamed all over the firm muscle of his chest and shoulders, and she'd dared to slip her hands under his t-shirt to caress the planes of his back.

"Stop it," she muttered to herself.

"Beg pardon?" Jessica, her tech said, puzzled. They were checking the old dog as she came out of the anesthesia.

"Sorry, thinking," she said, smiling at the young woman.

She couldn't afford to be distracted by thoughts of Dan Nutter. Not while she still had patients to see.

Just how much does he work out to have that amazing chest?

Annoyed with herself for her continued distraction, Adele shut down that avenue of thought. She'd just finished her latest appointment—and was now covered in slobber from Leif, the nervous Newfounland––when one of the technicians put her head in the door.

"Dr. Picard," she said. "There's two guys here who say they're from the FBI to see you. As soon as possible, they said."

"FBI!?" Adele exclaimed. She stripped off her gloves, and soiled lab coat, pulling on a clean white coat with her name embroidered over the pocket. After running a hand through her hair, she walked into the lobby. Two men stood there. They looked so stereotypically *federal*, in their dark glasses and dark suits, that Adele had to fight a smile.

"Good afternoon, gentlemen," she said, putting out her hand. "I'm Dr. Adele Picard. What can I do for you?"

The first man glanced at the obviously curious patrons. "Could we talk in private, Ms...I mean Dr. Picard?"

"Certainly, Mr...?"

"Special Agent Suarez, Dr. Picard. This is Lt. Emerson from the Massachusetts State Police."

The names sounded familiar, but she couldn't place them. She was pretty sure they were too young to have been involved with her case, seven years ago.

"Come on back." Adele led the way to her office, away from prying eyes. She pulled her office door closed. It gave an almighty creak because she almost never shut it. Moving behind her desk, she said, "Before I get you a cup of coffee or a cold drink, gentleman, may I see some ID?"

The two men shared another *look*, but they both produced the requested identification, giving her an unsubtle glance at the weapons they each carried in shoulder holsters. "Okay," she said, handing back their IDs, "Coffee? Something cold?"

"Thank you, no. Dr. Picard," Agent Suarez started. "You placed a call to the HomeSafePets this morning."

Well shit on a stick! This was about the dog.

In her pocket, her cell phone beeped with three incoming texts. She sighed. "I'm sorry. If you'll give me a moment? I have three patients on my emergency watch." She checked her phone.

They nodded in unison, as if they'd practiced it.

"I'll be right back."

Adele was glad she'd left the room because while the first two texts were from pet owners, the second was from Dan.

She returned the texts to Mimi's owner and the owner of a dog boarding at the clinic before opening the text from Dan. There, on her screen, was a smiley emoticon with z's coming out of its head.

Dan: Hey! Hope you got some sleep with all the insanity last night. It isn't even a full moon. He punctuated the end of the sentence with a moon emoticon.

The second text was more personal.

Dan: Despite the desperate nature of our meet-up last night, I enjoyed spending time with you. You never answered my question about a date. How about dinner tonight? Old Haven Mill Tavern? Judges

Chambers? Mike's?—Your choice!

And last but not least, the final text was about the dog.

Dan: Hope our patient is okay. I thought about it after I got home. I think he might be a guard or drug dog. Do you want me to put out some feelers with people I know in law enforcement?

Now that was interesting. She'd have pegged Jake Strongbow for that question, not Dan. What connection did Dan have with law enforcement?

Adele: Thank you for the offer. I'd really like dinner. Old Haven Mill Tavern is great. I love their burgers? And the FBI is here about the dog, so whatever your hunch might have been, it was probably on the mark. Do you think they told Chief Strongbow or the Sheriff that they're here?

Dan: The FBI? Do you want me to come over?

Adele: Agent Suarez from the FBI and Lt. Emerson from the State Police.

Dan: Those are the guys who were here for the murders around The Witches Walk. Interesting. Need backup? Want me to tell Jake?

Adele: Thanks, but I'm okay. Yes, I'd be happy for you to tell Jake.

Dan: Done. So, shall I pick you up at seven?

Adele: I'll drive over to Old Haven Mill Tavern. I might need to leave if I get an emergency.

Dan: Understood. See you at Old Haven Mill

Tavern.

Warmed to her toes, she wondered if he knew how much it meant that he'd offered to back her up. No one had done that in a long time. Then again, the last time she'd had someone step into the breech for her, he'd gotten himself killed.

The faint tug of grief for her late husband twinged, as it always did. Jeremy had been dead seven years, but she felt the sorrow try to invade.

"I've let it go. It's long past time to move on," she said, as she dropped the phone back into her pocket. She returned to her office. "Thank you for your patience. Now, why do I get the FBI and the State Police instead of his owners, who, by the way deserve a good tongue-lashing for letting such a valuable animal run loose?"

"He wasn't running loose," Emerson replied curtly. "It's more complicated than that. We'll get into it, but first, why don't you tell us what happened when you found him? Start with where, please."

Intrigued, Adele complied. "I'd been over the bridge, in Merrimack County, helping another vet out with a foaling draft horse. I headed home around one-thirty. It was raining, and I was having trouble staying

30

awake." She stopped to gather her thoughts. "I crested the hill about a mile before the bridge. The dog was in the road. I barely managed to stop before I hit him." The minute she paused, Suarez pounced on the information, grilling her about the time, place, and what she had seen.

"Yes, I saw taillights up in the distance. No, I didn't think anything of it until I came upon the dog." She paused, considering. "I'll bet they were the creeps who ditched him. He can't have been there too long."

"Were the taillights far apart and high, like a truck or SUV? Or closer together and lower, like a car?" Emerson latched onto the news that she'd seen a vehicle.

"Hmmm, I don't know. Hang on." Adele closed her eyes to better visualize what she'd seen. Her mind was still foggy with fatigue, but she was able to call the picture of the lights into her mind. "Higher up, like a truck, van or SUV," she finally said, wanting nothing more than to leave her eyes closed and sink into sleep. That was a far-off dream, however, so she opened her eyes and refocused on the two men across from her.

"Gentlemen, I've told you what I know. Now, what's going on? I certainly didn't expect you to be here this afternoon. You still haven't told me about his owners, and I have scheduled clients waiting." Through the glass in the office door, she'd seen Darlene, her office manager, hovering frantically in the back room. Things must be piling up in the waiting room.

"Yes, of course. I think that's all we need for now. Thank you for your help. We'll just get the dog and get out of your way." This from Suarez.

Adele didn't bother to conceal her shock. "Not a chance in hell. Sorry, gentlemen," she said firmly. She repressed a smile when the two men looked nonplussed. "No patient of mine leaves this hospital before I'm sure he's well. It's also hospital policy with strays, especially an obviously valuable animal like that dog, that anyone wanting to pick up the dog must produce proof of ownership. Since I doubt he's your personal pet Agent Suarez, I'll need to see an AKC registration or some other documentation before I release him. And the bill needs to be paid."

"Ms. Picard, is this..."

"Really necessary?" Adele finished his sentence for him. "Yes Agent, as any good *Doctor* will tell you, it is." She paused watching them glance at each other uneasily. Certain they wouldn't know, she asked, "What's the dog's name?"

Neither agent even blinked. Nor did they answer. "Dr. Picard, if we return with the proper forms will you release the dog into our custody?"

Adele's face hardened into a mask. "No, Agent Suarez, I won't. Unless you own this dog, or have a court order, I won't release him to you at all." She rose and stood by the door. "Now, gentlemen, if you will excuse me, I have patients waiting."

"Very well, we'll get the necessary paperwork. Please, whatever you do, don't wash the dog. I need to send a technician to see if we can gather any evidence from it."

"Evidence?"

Suarez's look would have made a lesser woman quail, but she wasn't budging.

"You're correct in that he's a very valuable animal. His owner's been kidnapped," Emerson said, and Suarez scowled ferociously at him. "If you won't release him to us, please don't do anything else with him until our tech can examine him."

Suarez reluctantly nodded. "If you're willing to keep and treat him, Dr. Picard, I assure you the bill will be paid. We'll be in touch as soon as we can. Meanwhile, please keep any bedding or bandages which you might have used on him so the tech can examine those as well."

Within a few minutes, and with several more admonitions to keep any information about the dog private, Adele watched them leave.

What the hell? It isn't even Halloween yet and I've got spooks and mysteries.

She leaned her head against the doorframe, letting the cool metal soothe her tired brain. She fought the familiar trapped feeling that she always felt around official cop-types. Oddly enough, neither Jake, nor the sheriff made her feel that way.

Growing up as the daughter of a prominent Southern senator, she'd had her fill of secret service and FBI types. Her late husband had been a lobbyist and she hated all the secrecy and the guards. Jeremy secrets had nearly killed them both.

Her tech, Jessica, roused her from her memories. "Doc, we've got two in the exam rooms and two waiting."

"Coming!"

Adele put the episode behind her and spent the afternoon giving shots, removing the sutures on a neuter, and reassuring Mrs. Lafayette again that Mimi was doing great as a first time mom. She checked in on the big

Shepherd several times, and each time he seemed more alert and curious. He wasn't at all aggressive, letting the techs open the cage and put a food bowl into his kennel. She brought him out just before they closed up, and took out the IV. He was the perfect gentleman through the whole procedure.

"This is one nice dog, Doc," Jessica said, opening the door to the kennel again and setting down a larger evening meal for the dog. Adele helped the big dog back into the crate and latched the door.

"He's obviously crate trained too."

Her phone pinged and she smiled. For the first time in a long time, she had a date.

Together, they closed up and Adele watched as Jessica got to her car, then locked the door to the clinic. Compelled to check on the dog one last time, Adele went into the back. The Shepherd was awake and alert and the bandage across his head gave him a piratical air. As Adele neared, his bandaged tail thumped and slithered against the hard plastic of the kennel. Adele squatted down and spoke to him.

"You're looking a little better than you did last night."

When talking to an animal one on one, Adele always made a mental picture of what she was saying or asking. She fit in in Haven Harbor, a town of witches and renegades, because in most cases, she could communicate with the animals that came into her clinic. She'd never told anyone about it, but she felt at home here because she was pretty sure no one in Haven Harbor would bat an eye even if they did find out.

"All right, sweet boy, here's what's going on. You're with me, you've been asleep." She pictured him lying in the road. "What happened?"

The dog growled and stood up, head down, teeth showing.

"Okay, something bad."

The dog shook, settling his ruffled fur back along his body before sitting back down again. She couldn't always understand what came back to her from the animals, usually only the emotions, but this time, a clear picture of flashing teeth, and two men shot into her mind. The satisfaction that the dog felt, in terms of biting the men, was clear.

This was the first time images of that clarity had come through. She looked at the dog in surprise.

"Well you're a whole different level of smart, aren't you?"

The dog shook again, and another picture

came through. A girl, blonde and petite, with fragile features and an elfin smile.

"That's your girl?"

In answer the dog whined, turned around three times, and lay down. Somehow Adele knew that the girl was in trouble and that the dog had tried and tried to save her, but had been knocked unconscious by the two men.

"That's a different kettle of fish, now isn't it?" she murmured, thinking hard about the FBI visit. This put a different spin on things. And yet, she didn't know what she could do about it, given that her information came from a reliable, but four-legged witness. "You get some rest. I'll be back in the morning."

The dog whined softly again.

"A mystery indeed," she said as she stood up. She checked her phone when it pinged again, and grinned.

Dan: Table at Old Haven Mill Tavern waiting just for you. I have an Eye of Newt burger ordered. George said it was your favorite.

Adele: On my way.

Dan: Looking forward to seeing you.

Suddenly they'd gone from edging around one another to a date. Finally. Adele locked up and set the alarm. Hurrying to her truck, she headed for Old Haven Mill Tavern.

CHAPTER TWO

Adele enjoyed the quick drive through the brightly decorated town and turned into the spookily decorated Old Haven Mill Tavern. As she walked in the door, the statuesque bartender, Mary-George McBride––who always went by just George—caught her eye.

Lifting a cold Ghostly Harbor IPA in a chilled mug, George pointed at it. Adele nodded vigorously and gave a thumbs up before heading to the table where Dan was waiting. He stood up to hold her chair, like a proper gentleman, which would've made Adele's southern mother jump with joy. In her weekly calls, Adele's mother bemoaned the fact that Adele wasn't meeting any *good men* up in Massachusetts, just *damn Yankees*.

Her mother missed the fact that Adele wasn't dating anyone at all.

And yet, now that she was on a date, somehow Adele couldn't visualize anyone more suitable than the tall, lanky, gorgeous man standing in front of her.

"Hey," Dan said, as he helped her out of her jacket. "How was your day?" She felt the brush of his fingers across the nape of her neck and very nearly sighed. Damn, the man had serious heat to him, even with just a touch.

"Hey back, it was pretty good." She sat, and waved at George as the server set the IPA in front of her. "Thanks. How's it going tonight Benita?"

Benita smiled, but her eyes were on Dan. "Good, thanks. Your food will be right out."

The young woman left the table, only to come right back with two large plates. She set the giant Eye of Newt burger in front of Adele before putting a Bubbling Trouble burger in front of Dan.

"Thank you," Adele said as she unfolded her napkin and nearly drooled over the burger. She'd grabbed a couple of protein bars during the day, and finished a leftover salad on the fly, after the rush this afternoon, but this was the first solid meal she'd sat down to for two days.

"I'm glad you weren't too tired to come out." He was watching her intently. "And I'm hoping you'll be willing to do it again. Soon."

"We haven't even gotten through this date and you want another?" she said, keeping it light. "Don't you want to hedge your bets?"

He was still watching her with that total focus. Dan had a way of looking at her, as if he was shutting everything else out, and it was only the two of them that mattered.

"No."

She couldn't think of anything witty to say, so she took a drink of the IPA.

With a smile, he picked up his burger and took a substantial bite. Not knowing what to say, or how to react to the sheer animal magnetism he exuded, she picked up her own burger. Biting in, she moaned.

"Oh, Gods, that's good."

His gaze zeroed in on her. There was hunger when he looked at her now, and he flicked a long finger out to catch a drop of ketchup off her lip. Eyes locked with hers, he brought the finger to his mouth, and licked off the ketchup.

"It's good," he said.

Lordy-dee, the man was trouble. For the first

time in years, Adele wanted some of that kind of sensual, sexual trouble. With him.

"How's the Bubbling Trouble?" another young server asked Dan, stopping at the table to refill their water glasses.

"Excellent," Dan said without ever breaking eye contact with Adele.

Adele smiled and managed to shift her gaze. The teenager wasn't paying any attention to Adele, of course, just like Benita. The girl was staring at Dan with that *OMG he's hot!* look in her eyes.

"We're fine," she said, with a bit more force than she'd intended. The girl blushed and moved along. Dan laughed.

"Territorial?"

She looked back at him, and decided to take a chance. "I don't share. You okay with that?"

Fire lit in the back of Dan's eyes and he reached over to slide a finger down the back of Adele's hand. "I'm honored."

Somehow the admissions, on both their parts, broke the sensual tension. A wild laugh from the bar area and the sight of a drink frothing over chased away any stiffness—even the sensual kind—they might have had. They joined in the applause as the patron tossed back the smoking beverage, evidently on a dare, and returned to their burgers.

The conversation flew from topic to topic and Adele realized she was having a great time. In the meantime, she'd also polished off the burger, the fries and the pickle wedge without tasting hardly any of it. She was so tuned into Dan it was almost painful.

Unfortunately, a full belly, and the warm room hit her with the force of a freight train. All of a sudden, an enormous yawn threatened to crack her jaw.

"Oh, wow, sorry. It isn't the company, I assure you," she said, embarrassed.

He reached out to toy with her fingers where they lay on the tablecloth, and she felt her body react. Heat headed right for her belly and it was all she could do to sit still and act normally.

"I'm glad," he frowned. "How much sleep have you actually managed in the last few days?"

"About four hours."

"You should have told me," he said, his frown deepening. "We could have gone out Friday instead."

"Are you asking me for a second date?" she said, trying to ease the frown, and hoping she wasn't being too forward.

A variety of emotions ran over his features,

and she wondered if she'd made a mistake, but the smile returned and he said, "Name the time and place."

"Let me sleep on it, but I'd love to go out again, when I have a few more functioning brain cells."

"Great," he said, putting several bills into the leatherette folder the waitress had left with yet one more soulful look at Dan. "I'll walk you to your car."

She unlocked her door with a quick beep, and turned to say goodnight. Before she could utter a word, his mouth was on hers. Hot and passionate, the kiss took her off guard, but she caught up quickly. The meshing of tongues and the way his hands gripped her hips made her ache with need.

A car honked as it sped down River Road, and someone yelled out, "Wooohooo! Get it on, Mr. Nutter!"

They broke apart, and Adele laughed breathlessly. "Oh, Lord, Mr. Nutter? Do all the library patrons know you?" She said, trying to calm her racing heart and surging hormones. She wanted to drag him into the back of her truck and take wicked advantage of him. Right now.

He rested his forehead against hers. "I manage the high school library as well as the town library. A strange arrangement, but it works in Haven Harbor." He bent to brush his lips over hers again. "If you weren't so tired and this wasn't a first date," he said, his voice trailing off.

"I know. But…" she said, enjoying the warmth of him almost as much as his kisses.

"Friday night?"

"Yeah," she said. "But I'll see you at the regular Coven meeting tomorrow, right?"

"With bells on," he quipped. He kissed her again, just the merest brush of lips on lips. It was tantalizing. He'd done that at the clinic and the move aroused her to a fever pitch. "Will you be all right driving home?"

"Uh-huh," she murmured, sliding her hands into his hair to draw him closer.

"Okay." He deepened the kiss and pulled her in tight. His body was so hot, so fiery and wonderful, that she wanted to run her hands– –hell, her tongue and her lips—all over it.

"I don't know what you're thinking, but I can guess," he said, a growl in his voice. "And I approve. Wholeheartedly."

"I'm so glad," she admitted, laughing. She widened the gap between them. The cool night air did nothing to tamp her desire, but, even though they knew each other, it was a first date, and she was exhausted. Much as she wanted him to follow her home, she wanted to be able to keep up her part of what promised to be an outstanding romp once they did get together.

She was pretty sure that was going to happen. She grinned. For the first time in years, she was ready.

"Good night, Dan," she said, letting his hair slide through her fingers, and drop to rest on his chest. "I'll see you Friday."

He stepped back and the cool October air shivered between them. She crossed her arms over her chest and his eyes zeroed in on the movement. She laughed, a little breathlessly.

"Friday," he said, and stepped back, opening her door. Once again, he watched her drive away.

Dan went to the gym. He knew if he went home that he'd end up reliving every minute of his time with Adele. He grinned. Not that it would be a bad thing, but it would lead to even more frustration than he was currently feeling. Striding into the echoing building, which, even in its utilitarian plainness, was decorated with Halloween lights and pumpkins, Dan headed straight for the lift rack, loading on extra plates before setting up to lift.

"Hey man, what're you doing here so late?" Jake strolled over from the little kitchen area, run on the honor system, swilling a Gatorade.

Dan jerked the weight up and settled it on his shoulders before answering. "Working off some frustration. You?"

Chief of Haven Harbor's small police department, Jake Strongbow, his lean face drawn, arched his back in a stretch before he sat down on a nearby weight bench. He didn't answer the question. Instead, he posed another of his own. "What's got you frustrated?"

"Adele."

"When are you going to finally ask her out?" Jake yawned, and Dan answered it with a yawn of his own.

"Stop that. We had our first date tonight."

Jake grinned and wiggled his eyebrows. "Tell me more."

"Yeah, yeah. I don't kiss and tell. I'm tired but I need to lift and get some of this energy out."

"Oh, that kind of frustration," Jake smirked and when Dan shot him a glare, he laughed out loud. "So you heard the Suarez and Emerson are back, and they want the dog she found, right?"

"Yeah. Adele wouldn't turn him over."

46

"Her clinic, her rules. They'll be back."

"When?" Dan asked, settling the bar back into the rack. "I want to be there."

"I'll let you know, since I plan to be there too. I'm not fond of the feds or the state boys coming in here without telling me first."

"I thought you liked Suarez and Emerson, after what happened last month. You said they were pretty good, for state and fed wonks." Dan knew that the two men had been pretty helpful in solving the murders during the days leading up to the annual Witches Walk.

"And they are. Still. My town." Jake looked grim.

"Yeah. My woman. So let me know."

"Does she know that? About her being your woman?" Jake yawned again.

"If she doesn't, I hope she will after another few dates," Dan said, preparing the weights for the next lift.

Jake just gave him a look. "We'll see, I guess. Keep your phone on. I caught Suarez by phone finally. Off the record, the dog's tied to a kidnapping. It's radio silent to keep it out of the news, so keep it buttoned up. Don't know if whoever's doing this wants the dog too, but just in case."

"More reason for me to be there with her,"

Dan said. Switching to free weights, he smoothly curled them up and down, working his biceps, then his shoulders. They sat in companionable silence as Dan moved to both chest and leg presses.

When he'd done three sets, he began to feel the tension loosening. Maybe now he could sleep without a pulsing hard-on keeping him awake.

"I'm heading out," Jake said. "You'll lock up?"

"Yeah. When're we getting together for poker again?"

"Saturday night. You in? Or you taking your lady out for Saturday too?" Jake grinned at him and laughed when Dan shot him the finger.

"I don't know if she'll go again that soon, so count me in. For now. If she will, I'm totally ditching you ugly mutts."

"For now," Jake answered, slinging a towel around his neck and jingling the set of keys he'd just picked up. "Let me know if you wanna catch dinner and the game on Sunday."

"You're on."

"'Night," Jake said, walking toward the door. He tapped a glowing pumpkin on a stand as he passed and the motion activated prop let out a spooky laugh.

"'Night," Dan answered, watching his friend disappear into the darkness.

He was worried about Jake. Most of the town was. Susan, Jake's wife, had packed and moved out the day after the Witches Walk. Even with his best friends, Jake had been stoic and silent about his personal life. Nothing new there, but for different reasons.

When the separation papers had come by courier just days later, he'd said nothing. He hadn't talked to them, and he hadn't gotten an attorney. He'd just signed the papers and sent them back to the Boston lawyer Susan had hired.

Alone in the gym, Dan sat down on another bench and readied himself for the next couple of sets. He'd just gripped the weights when he felt a chill.

"Hello, Daniel," a cheery voice spoke out of nothingness. Within a few minutes, a misty form came into being and hovered over the other bench.

"Hello Great-Grandma Nutter." The ghosts of his ancestors seemed to find it normal to pop in anytime and chat with him. He wasn't a medium. No other ghosts bothered him. Just his ancestors. Although his ghosts apparently talked with other ghosts, Dan never saw anyone but his own kin.

"So you took my advice and went out to the Mouldon road last night."

"I did. Thank you for the information." It seemed like forever ago, rather than just the previous evening.

She waved a misty hand. "Of course. The little gal needed help, obviously. And she has a crush on you. You know that, right?"

He cursed the blush that came from nowhere and heated his face. It was one thing to kiss Adele and want her as badly as he did. It was another to have his Great-Grandmother start talking about Adele and how she might feel about him.

"You like her, don't you?" Great-Grandma Nutter persisted. "You've never been reluctant where women were concerned, boy. Not got the jitters do you?"

"No, ma'am." He gritted his teeth against the surge of embarrassment for the questioning, and lifted, counting the reps in his head.

"Good. Now, you be over there to her place first thing in the morning. She'll need you then too."

"Her house?" Dan froze, settled the weights back into their place. How would he explain showing up at her house? "Why? What's going on? What did you learn?"

"No, silly," she said, as she started to fade out. "Her business. Just be there."

"Dammit," he cursed. If they had to bother him and interfere in his life, the least the ghosts could do is give him enough information to actually help.

He tried to do another set, but realized he was done for the night. He texted Jake before he pulled out of the parking lot.

He started the text with the ghost emoji.

Dan: Hey dude, They *told me to be at the clinic first thing in the morning. Probably means you should be too.*

Jake: Got it. See you there.

####

After a great meal in superb company, and nine hours of solid, uninterrupted sleep, Adele felt like a new woman. She'd gotten into the clinic just after dawn. She loved getting an early start. She let her two dogs out into the kennel yard behind the clinic then headed in to see the Shepherd

"Let's take a look at you this morning. Will you let me get you up on the table?" She opened the kennel door and waited. When he cocked his head in what she'd come to think of his pirate pose, he looked ridiculous. She laughed. "Silly pup. You know you're cute, don't you? So, how about it? Let's check that tail."

The dog cocked his head, ears pricked, listening to her words. Adele decided to give it a chance. She had a good feeling about his temperament, and trusted her gut.

"Okay, pup. Let's go slow."

The dog rose and eased out the door. On a hunch, Adele walked over to the exam table and patted it. "Up here, boy. Let's take a look at you."

The dog limped over to the where she stood and looked at her. She patted the table again. Despite being a little wobbly, the dog barely hesitated before leaping up onto the exam table. She caught him as he staggered, steadying him.

"Not too steady. That's not good. No more jumping, then. I'm thinking that head wound is from someone cracking you over the noggin with something," she said to the pup as she checked his pupillary response. It was just fractionally slow, which could indeed mean a concussion. Without other symptoms, or an owner's permission, she didn't want to do any other tests. "Just because it isn't cracked though," she said to the dog, "Doesn't mean your skull isn't bruise or concussed."

She patted his side. In the bright morning

light spilling through the windows to augment the clinic lights, Adele could see this was indeed a well-cared for animal. Underneath the dirt from the road, she could tell the dog's coat was healthy. His nails well-trimmed and he was clean at the skin level—no rough patches in his fur, and no fleas. Judging from his teeth, also pristinely white, he was four to five years old. He also had impeccable manners. The dog lay like a statue as Adele removed the tape on his tail and examined her handiwork.

There was swelling, of course, and some discharge, but Adele was sure that the dog's tail had been deliberately sliced off. She'd had to remove an additional vertebrae in his tail in order to close the wound. She could only hope that it would heal well. Tail wounds were challenging, because a happy dog moved his tail a lot. Every time a dog wagged, they risked opening the wound, and there was no way to immobilize it.

With steady hands and a renewed fury for whoever had done this, she put a new dressing on the tail, wrapping it well. She looked the dog in the eye, saying, "Now don't chew on that."

The dog's quizzical expression made her laugh.

A knock on the clinic door transformed the Shepherd from a comic rogue into an instantly alert, working guard. His hackles raised and he jumped off the table in a heartbeat. Despite the distinct wobble in his step, he positioned himself in front of Adele.

"It's okay, boy. Sit." The dog just looked at her. Adele searched her mind for the hand signal for *sit*. When she gave it, the dog sat. Then the signal to *stay*. Adele crossed her fingers that she'd done it right. "Gotta call Rebecca," she muttered. Her friend from vet school trained companion dogs. "I need the name of a good book on working dogs if he's going to be hanging out for any length of time."

Thank goodness the hand signals were universal. She better get a few other commands down so rover-boy didn't take a hunk out anyone.

The knocking had continued as she got the dog settled. She looked through the security peep, something she probably wouldn't have done before the last Witches Walk and all the trouble.

Seven people stood outside in the bright October morning. Sheriff Carl Lackner, and Chief Jake Strongbow she recognized, of course. And Dan. She smiled at him before she turned to greet the others. The agents she'd already met made two more, but the rest were new.

Two others, a man and a woman, were obviously also agents and Adele pretty much forgot them as soon as they were introduced because the final man drew all of her attention. He looked haggard and his expression was bleak. He was tall, with broad shoulders slumped in weariness. His caramel-colored hair fell carelessly into his eyes.

Those eyes cleared when he looked at her. When they focused in, they were scalpel sharp and a compelling, steely grey. Unusual. And anger rode hard underneath the pain, a fact Adele discovered when he looked at her.

Agent Suarez stepped forward. "Dr. Picard," he said, formally. "This is Dr. Thomas Spradling, the owner of the dog."

Adele nodded and motioned for the group to follow her inside. As they rounded the corner into the kennel area, the dog whined but kept his seat. The man's shoulders came up and he dropped to one knee. Adele released the dog from the sit-stay, and he bounded to the man. The smile on Thomas Spradling's face changed it into startling handsomeness.

"Hatter!" he exclaimed, greeting the ecstatic

dog. Tears rolled heedlessly down his face and the dog licked at them and anything else he could reach. Adele fought her own emotions at the reunion.

After a few moments, the man put Hatter into a sit, much in the same way Adele had done. When he stood, he wiped his eyes on his sleeve. The momentary weakness was erased by the gesture. When he dropped his arm his face was once more unreadable. With Hatter plastered to his side, Thomas extended his hand and Adele shook it firmly.

"I can't thank you enough for all that you've done for Hatter." He glanced at the Agents. "If you have somewhere private we can talk, Dr. Picard, I'll show you his papers and settle his bill."

"If you'll follow me, I'll tell you about Hatter. Then we'll talk about the bill."

The agents made as if to follow the two into Adele's office, but Thomas Spradling forestalled them. "I'll talk with Doctor Picard privately."

"Right in here, Dr. Spradling," Adele said. "Dan? Would you join us?"

Dan stepped forward, and she nodded at Jake and Carl. "Gentlemen, we'll be with you in a moment."

Dan and Thomas Spradling followed her

into the neat office with Hatter still plastered to Thomas's side. Dan pushed the door and it swung closed with its usual creak.

To hide her nervous reaction to Dan's presence, Adele moved behind the desk and straightened some papers, before sitting. Dan had moved to stand at her side, supporting her. Adele asked him to come in with her because he'd been there too. When his hand rested lightly, warmly on her shoulder, it made her smile. She returned her gaze to Thomas. "Please, have a seat Dr. Spradling."

"Call me Thomas," he replied, then, with a small smile added, "You say Dr. Spradling and I look for my father." As he sat, he fished in the breast pocket of his suit and came out with a windowed envelope. The return address was for the American Kennel Club. "There's Hatter's legal registration and here," he pulled out his wallet, "is my driver's license that proves I'm who I say I am."

She didn't take the documents right away. She looked into his eyes. "I don't really need to see your ID, Dr. Sp...Thomas. Hatter's reaction to you was proof enough of ownership. But, before you put them away," she reached for the AKC papers, "I would like to see what his breeding is."

He handed over the envelope. The

pedigree inside confirmed what she had thought. This dog was not only purebred he was extremely well-bred. She grinned at Hatter's owner. "I told my tech that this dog had Top Hat kennels in his bloodline." She put the papers back in the envelope. "Even with his injuries, style is just written all over him."

"Thank you, Dr. Picard." he began. "I tried to get the best possible breeding and training in a dog. Hatter is my daughter's constant companion."

Adele frowned and started to speak, he held up a hand to forestall her. Dan moved closer. The contact warmed her to her toes, in spite of the cold ball of dread that settled in her gut when Thomas mentioned his daughter. The strain on his face told Adele something was very, very wrong.

"The reason for all the secrecy is that my daughter was kidnapped two days ago and Hatter disappeared with her." He stopped, struggled for a moment then cleared his throat and continued. "By FedEx I received a ransom note and...and the end of Hatter's tail." His hand stroked the dog's unbandaged ears and Hatter leaned his full weight against his master's knee, pushing into the caress.

Adele's heart clenched in her chest. Her

breath backed up in her lungs until it was impossible to breathe.

"The kidnappers drugged everyone in the house while I was at a dinner meeting. My housekeeper is still in the hospital. Gabrielle," he stopped, emotion flooding his voice.

Dan's hand squeezed Adele's shoulder and their eyes met as they gave Thomas a moment to recover. She gulped in some air. It struck her as intimate and connected that he would be there. He didn't know about what had happened to her, but if this how supportive he was she was half in love with him already.

The thought disturbed her enough that she moved out from under Dan's hand, and shifted her chair to the little fridge in the credenza. She handed Thomas a bottle of water, and pushed the box of tissue across the desk.

He opened the water and drank, then continued. "Thank you. When the call came from HomeSafePets, we assumed the worst. Agent Suarez headed here right away. He said he knew this town. He came to recover Hatter and get information from you." Thomas actually managed another small smile. "They found you too tough, I gather."

Adele returned the smile. "I guess. Hatter was injured, and that puts him first."

Thomas glanced at Dan, then cleared his throat again. "I'm glad you were the one to find him."

"Dan was with me. That's one of the reasons I wanted him to be here." Thomas nodded and she continued. "Hatter was left in the middle of the road."

"Oh, my God." He turned to run his hands over the dog, before swiveling back to face her. "Was he hit? Is he going to be okay?"

"He wasn't hit by a car, but I think he was hit over the head. I'm worried about that blow, and a possible concussion. The wound on his tail is serious as well. Now that I know that his tail was actually cut, it makes sense." She took a deep breath before she continued. "I found Hatter before anyone hit him, but," she said, reaching up for Dan's hand as she said the next words. "Whoever dumped him intended for him to be killed. If I hadn't been driving slowly I wouldn't have been able to stop in time. I would have run over him."

She couldn't help the shudder that flew up her spine. She'd thought about that in the dark hours of the night as she sat with the Lafayette's poodle. She'd have killed Hatter if she'd been going her usual break-neck pace. And, had Dan not come, she might not have been able to get Hatter into the truck or into the clinic.

"Thomas," Dan spoke for the first time. "I know you don't know us, but if there's any way we can help, I hope you'll call on us."

"Thank you. I know Agent Suarez has asked that Hatter be processed, whatever that means. They're not hopeful that he's retained any evidence, but they'll still do it. Does he still need to be under a doctor's care?"

Adele frowned, thinking. Something was niggling at her. If he had a vet for Hatter to go to in Boston, she'd have to release Hatter to him. But she *knew* the dog needed to stay in her care. Whenever she went against her gut, bad things happened, so she followed that hunch, followed that feeling whenever she could.

"If he were one of my regular patients, I'd insist he stay here for observation for at least one more night. Both the tail and the head wound need to be monitored. If you insist on taking him home today, I need your promise that your regular vet will do that."

Thomas shook his head. "Our vet is out of the country at some kind of conference. Would you be willing to treat him for now? I'll pay the boarding fee or whatever you need. I want him to be well when we," he stopped, emotion tightening his features. "When we bring Gabrielle home. She'll need him even more."

"Of course." Relief surged through her. Whatever Hatter had to do, or whatever she had to do for Hatter, it was going to work out, because she was keeping him. At the same time, she worried about Thomas Spradling. She could only imagine what a parent went through when a child was taken. She'd been an adult when she and Jeremy had been grabbed in Mexico, but she knew her parent had still suffered agonies until she'd been rescued. And shared her grief when Jeremy hadn't made it.

She pushed her own issues into the background as they all stood. Thomas shook hands with Dan and with Adele. "I'll give you daily updates once I have your information, Thomas."

"Good. Then let's rejoin the others," Thomas said, and Adele saw the shadow of the man he usually was. A man used to giving orders and having them instantly obeyed. Suarez had said he ran a multinational biopharmaceutical firm in Boston. Now, he was grieving, afraid, and out of his depth because he wasn't in control of anything. His daughter was missing and he couldn't ride to the rescue.

Adele's father had never recovered from his need to over-protect his only child. His concern had been welcome when she was grieving. As she recovered, however, well… There was a reason her dad lived in South Carolina and Adele lived in the most northern part of Massachusetts.

Jake was the first to speak when the three of them left Adele's office. "Dr. Picard, Missy's here from my office to process the dog for any evidence."

"Great. Let's get him on the exam table." She turned to Thomas. "This will be easier now that I know his name."

"If you want him to jump up, just tell him Hatter, up," Thomas said, patting the table as Adele had done earlier. Before Adele could forestall him, the dog sprang to the table so lightly, it was as if he'd levitated. Once again, however, he was just the slightest bit wobbly.

Adele caught the dog. "I was going to lift him, this time," she explained. "I'm worried his balance is off due to the head wound."

Missy, the crime technician from Jake's office had arrived. She squeaked a little as the dog seemed to just appear on the table.

"Wow. That is one huge dog." Her eyes were like saucers. In an instant, Adele realized the young woman was afraid of Hatter.

"I'll stand here at his head," Adele said, moving in front of the dog and burying her hands in the dog's ruff. "That will keep him focused on me. What do you need to do?"

"Comb out his fur, see if I can get anything useful. Hair that isn't his, wool or synthetic fibers from a coat, carpet fibers from whatever vehicle he was transported in."

"The blanket from the truck," Dan said, and she knew instantly what he meant. It would be more likely to have caught fibers from the dog's coat when they picked him up from the road.

"My keys are on the hook over there," she pointed to a row of metal hooks by the rear door. "The blanket's still in the back."

Missy handed Dan a paper bag. "Put it in this."

"There's a towel there," Adele said, pointing, and Missy bagged the towel from the kennel where Hatter had slept. Then, with sure strokes that betrayed none of the nervousness in her eyes, Missy combed through the dog's fur, catching any detritus onto stiff white paper as she went. She folded the hairs and dirt she collected into the papers and slid them each into a separate envelope. "That's it."

"I have his blood," Adele said, suddenly remembering that she'd drawn the vials, thinking to run a toxicological screening. "From when I brought him in. He was unconscious, but since the head wound wasn't as severe as I initially thought, I wondered if he'd been poisoned. Given what Dr. Spradling said, I'm thinking maybe he was drugged."

Missy brightened at the word *blood* and Adele suppressed a grin. Science geeks were so alike. In equal geekery, she'd been thrilled to watch the methodology of collecting forensic evidence.

They'd just wrapped up when the back door opened and Adele's tech and office manager came in to start the day. To a woman, they stopped to stare at the odd collection of people in the usually empty back room.

"Uh, good morning, Dr. Picard," Darlene finally said. "I see we have company. Should I start some coffee?"

"Sound's good, Darlene. Michelle, if you'll start rounds, I'll be with you in a few minutes. Jessica, I know you finished everything last night on the testing for the Harper's cat, but if you could be sure the results got to the lab?"

"Sure thing, Doc," Michelle said, flicking

furtive glances at everyone as she put her things away and moved to the first kennel in the room. Adele didn't intend to introduce anyone, since Emerson had said that everything about the Spradling case was being kept quiet. Jessica and Darlene just smiled and got to work.

"Gentlemen, I've told Thomas that Hatter needs to stay at least for a day or two so I can keep an eye on his wounds. I'm concerned about a concussion, and about the tail healing properly. However, I'm available for any questions you might have, or if I can be of any help."

Suarez stepped forward to hand her a card. "I'll be in touch if we have more questions about the car you saw."

She nodded, and shook his hand. He moved to Dan, and shook his hand as well. "Mr. Nutter, thank you for the information you provided. You've given us a solid lead."

Adele shot him a look. When had Suarez talked to Dan? And what did Dan know? They'd been so busy, so focused on the heat between them at the Tavern, that she hadn't asked him what he'd been able to tell Suarez and Emerson. She'd have to rectify that.

Jake and Dan shook hands and the sheriff and the state and federal officers stepped out the clinic door, presumably to talk without being overheard. Jake followed them out, so that Dan, Thomas, and Adele were alone once more.

"Thank you for looking after Hatter. I'll be in touch as well."

"If there's anything you can provide him, something of your daughter's maybe, to keep him settled? That would be great."

Beyond Thomas, Dan stood looking at her, his eyes narrowing in puzzlement. Again, she didn't know why, but she knew she needed something of the girl's to keep Hatter safe and stable.

"Yes, of course. I'll send a courier with the blanket that stays on the foot of her bed."

"Thank you."

She put Hatter back in his kennel, where the dog whined as his master left the room. "It's okay boy," she said, while simultaneously trying to reassure him on that odd mental wavelength she shared with her patients. He licked her fingers through the bars before settling down to put his long nose on his paws.

She caught Dan's look again, but he said nothing as the two of them followed the crowd out into the morning sunshine.

The sheriff was the first to leave, followed

by the dark sedan into which Suarez and Emerson had hustled Dr. Spradling. Jake stood by his sturdy, official Bronco, waiting for them.

"That was interesting," he drawled. He turned back to Adele. "What's the real reason you're keeping the dog?"

"He needs to be monitored," she said, keeping a straight face, though her heart was pounding. She'd never told anyone about her secret ability, and she really didn't know why she needed Hatter. Even though Haven Harbor welcomed the...unusual, and was a town of witches, Adele didn't trust anyone with the knowledge of what made her so different.

Dan moved to her side, his arm resting on her waist. It was a reassuring weight.

Jake looked at Dan, nodded, and shifted off the SUV's bumper. "I'd best be going. Missy'll want to know what to do with everything she's collected. Suarez'll be champing at the bit to get it all to his lab boys in Boston."

"What will they do now?" Adele asked. She'd been on the other side of this equation when she was kidnapped, so she could only assume.

"They've had a ransom request. Spradling

wants to pay it, of course. The Feds don't want him too. From all accounts it was a slick, professional operation. The only loose end seems to be the dog."

"Makes sense on both sides," she said.

"Yeah, but with a little girl in the middle, it's a toss up as to who'll win," Jake concluded. "Well, I'd best go."

"Talk to you soon," Dan said.

Jake nodded. "Adele. Dan. See you later." He left them with a two-fingered salute and a wave as he, too, pulled out of the lot.

Her mind flew back to the past. She and Jeremy had been on a one-year-anniversary trip they'd been taken. Her parents and Jeremy's had wanted to pay too, but the police moved in instead. In the fight, Jeremy and all the kidnappers had been killed.

Shaking off the memory, she pivoted to go back into the clinic. Dan stopped her with a word. "Adele?"

"Yes?" She smiled at him. He'd been so fabulous to be here, to stay.

"What aren't you telling them about the dog?"

CHAPTER THREE

"Nothing," Adele said.

Dan frowned. "Adele."

How could he infuse such meaning, just in her name? She huffed out a breath and he closed the small distance between them.

"What is it?"

She looked at him, thinking about trust, and support. Maybe it was time to give a little.

"I don't know. Just a feeling."

He nodded. He knew what it was like to *know* something—usually something one of his ghosts had told him—and not be able to say exactly what it was. He hadn't told her yet about the ghosts. Only his best friends knew. Jake called him a spirit-talker, but he didn't think that was the right term any more than medium was. Everyone knew he was a practicing witch in the main Haven Harbor Coven, but only his select few friends knew about his ancestors popping in and out of his life.

"I'm not some person off the street, Adele. I'm not going to look at you funny if there's something you know or some way you know, or even if it's just a hunch. As Jake is fond of saying," he changed his voice to mimic Jake's slow, New England drawl. "A hunch is as good as a letter around Haven Harbor."

Adele laughed, but it sounded a little breathless. "I know. It's just...weird."

Dan laughed. "Everyone around here's a little weird, Adele."

The clinic door opened and they drew apart. Darlene grinned at them, but said, "Doc, your phone's ringing and it's Mrs. Lafayette."

"Got it," she said, relieved that she didn't have to do the great confession in the parking lot. "Duty calls. See you at the Coven meeting?"

"Absolutely. Still on for dinner tomorrow night?" he said, pulling her in for a kiss as the door closed behind Darlene.

"Yeah," she answered and her voice was husky as their bodies connected.

"This time, I'll pick you up."

####

Adele endured the good natured teasing from both Darlene and her techs as the day went on. She got through everything she needed to do while checking on Hatter every so often. Her other patients came and went, with some being picked up and others being dropped for a long weekend's boarding.

She left at five to get home in time to get ready. It was always fun to go to the Coven Meetings. They usually did a ritual, calling power and sending it where it was needed. In this case, they were sending it to protect the town. The long-term Wards that surrounded and protected Haven Harbor and its citizens for centuries had been broken in September, right after The Witches Walk.

Everyone was still in shock over the news that those Wards actually existed. That kind of magick wasn't common, especially not in the twenty-first century. Almost everyone in the Coven had thought the Wards were a myth—a sort of catch-all of good will to which they sent energy and Light—rather than something real.

According to the still-recovering Estelle Hestworth, and their High Priestess, Lucille Birkland, Haven Harbor wouldn't be able to totally close the breech in the town's defenses until Yule. In the meantime, the Coven would renew the smaller wardings and work to mend the damage.

When the ritual was done, it was just like the pot luck dinners after church that Adele had loved as a child. She hadn't loved church, but she'd loved the fellowship of dinner on the grounds. In college, she'd found her way to witchcraft. Her heart and soul had felt comfortable and safe for the first time.

But oh, a pot luck! When you were single, and lived alone, it was wonderful to have the fabulous variety of foods. Everyone had brought a dish to share and all of them were delicious. There were so many of her favorite fall dishes, including pumpkin pie and apple tarts, as well fish fresh practically right off the boat. There was even one of Minnie Terwilliger's massive, famous peach confections which had, once again, won first prize at the fair.

Adele wasn't much of a cook, but she'd brought pumpkin swirl muffins, and they were going fast.

"Now Adele, I want you to take your dish and fill it up with leftovers," a voice said at her elbow. "Believe me, I know what it's like to live alone." Lucille Birkland, the high priestess, and lead witch of Haven Harbor, and one of the town's most well-respected bankers, held a half-filled dish of her own. "As you can see, I've got the last muffin and I'm going to do the same."

"Thank you," Adele said, taking up the now-empty plate from her muffins. Following Lucille's lead, she turned to fill it with leftovers.

"You too, Dan, Patty, and Mirelle," Lucille called. "Come fill a plate."

Dan sauntered over, his smile focused on Adele. He walked directly to her and bent to kiss her.

"Oh, now what's this?" Lucille cooed. "How lovely. You're seeing one another?"

Dan put his arm around Adele's shoulders. "She's agreed to go out with me, yes."

"Oh, I'm so glad." Lucille continued to beam.

Adele, blushing, filled her plate and covered it with foil. Dan did the same and when they were done, they headed for the coatroom. Dan set down his leftovers so he could take her jacket, holding it so she could slide into it.

Once again, she decided her mother would love his good manners, even if he wasn't a Southerner.

"Thank you."

He bent and kissed the nape of her neck. "I'm looking forward to our date," he murmured, as he straightened.

Heat sparked in her blood and settled into her belly. She wanted to grab him and draw him down for one of those hot, tangled kisses like they'd shared at the Tavern. However, others were starting to come toward them, aiming for their own coats. Several were smiling at them and she could see that the gossip tree was already in full swing.

"Are you headed home?" Dan asked as he escorted her to her car.

"No, I've got to go back to the clinic. Jessica needed the night off, so I'll take the night check on the dogs and cats that are in-house."

"Want company?"

Adele hesitated only for a moment. "Sure."

They agreed to ride together and then Adele would drop him back by to his car on her way home. In the warm confines of her truck, she wasn't sure what to say or how to act. It baffled her that he had that effect one her. Usually, she managed her few dates with a smooth, capable skill.

Something about Dan short-circuited her

game there.

"I don't know what to do with you," Adele blurted. As soon as the words left her mouth, she wished she could take them back. How stupid could she be?

He laughed. "What do you mean?" He turned his body toward her, his hand stretched along the back of the seat, letting his fingers play with the strands of her loose hair.

"You," she started, as she turned into the clinic lot, "are a complication."

"Complication?"

"Yeah," she admitted. "I like to keep my life simple."

She parked and they both got out. For a moment, he didn't speak and didn't come around the edge of the truck. A bitterly cold breeze hit her and she shivered. "Dan?"

"Adele, get behind the truck. There's someone in the clinic."

"Shit," she said, hustling around to the passenger side. "How do you know?"

"Saw a shadow across the window. A flashlight, maybe."

She frowned, looking at the building. The angle of the windows should've made that impossible.

"I'm calling Jake," he added, pulling her close as he tapped a number on his cell.

At that moment, she heard a sharp, yowling cry and every dog in the clinic began to bark and howl. The sound of crashing metal and breaking glass sounded from within.

"Oh, hell no," she declared. "I'll be freakin' damned if I let someone hurt my patients." Snarling in anger, she grabbed the baseball bat she kept in the bed of the truck and ran for the clinic door.

A siren whooped close by, but she wasn't going to wait and let anyone hurt the dogs and cats under her care.

"Adele, stop!" Dan yelled as he ran after her.

She'd nearly reached the door when it burst open and a man ran out with Ribald clinging to his back, hissing and clawing at the man's head. Adele swung the bat at the man's hip, driving him into the gravel of the lot, without endangering Ribald.

Leaping forward as Ribald jumped off, Dan pulled the man's hands behind his back and twisted them into a secure hold. She noticed and approved the move, even as she wondered how he knew it.

Seconds later, a cruiser pulled into the lot and Officer Jim Capen jumped out. Right behind him, Jake spewed gravel as he pulled in as well.

While the officers cuffed the man, Adele grabbed Ribald and wrapped him in her arms, striving to calm the furious feline.

"What's this, an attack cat?" Jake asked, as Dan got up.

"What the hell were you thinking?" Dan launched in on Adele the minute he was sure Capen had the burglar under control. "You could have been killed."

Adele looked dumbfounded. Then she snarled wordlessly at him, and turned on her heel without answering and stomped into the clinic.

"Whoa, whoa," Jake said, catching Dan's arm before he rushed in after Adele. "Take a breath and think, man. No one, especially a strong, independent woman, wants to be yelled at like that. Not when they've had a scare."

"Dammit." Dan stalked up and down the lot, running his hands through his hair. His heart had nearly stopped when she'd grabbed the bat and run for the door. But she'd had a scare too. Jake was right about that.

When Dan's many-times-great grandfather had popped into instant manifestation at the side of the car, chilling the air, he'd warning Dan that "his gel" would be in danger if she went into the clinic. Dan heart nearly stopped. He'd made up an excuse as fast as he could to get her back to the truck. He hadn't counted on her being totally pissed that someone was breaking into her business.

Nor had he anticipated that she'd go dashing in, bat in hand.

Jake was right, he'd been scared to death. For her.

Shit. He'd known Adele was important to him. He hadn't realized she's become *that* important.

"Got a grip now?" Jake said. "We need to get in there."

"Let's go."

The two men followed Adele into the clinic. She was kneeling on the floor, cradling Ribald and crying.

Dan rushed to her side. "Adele, what is it? Is he hurt? Are you hurt?"

"He's okay. I'm okay. It just hit me, that's all."

Dan did the right thing this time, and sat on the floor to gather her into his arms, cat and all. "I'm glad. I'm sorry I yelled. I was so scared for you." There, he'd said it.

She sniffled. "Thanks."

Jake handed down a box of tissue from the counter and rolled his eyes. Dan glared at him. "Here, love," he said, handing her a tissue, and taking another to pat at the tears on her checks. Ribald was purring so loudly in his joy at being held, it could probably be heard in the parking lot.

"Doesn't look like the guy got too far," Jake said, examining the room. There were things knocked off the counter, and the center, wheeled, stainless steel table was turned over, and across the room, but nothing else seemed out of place. Most of the dogs were finally calming, although Hatter and one other dog continued to growl and pace as best they could in their kennels. Ribald, on the other hand, seemed delighted to be snuggled between two warm humans. He settled right in and continued to purr.

"I'm going to go check your security panel, and your door," Jake said, leaving them alone.

"Hey, are you really okay?" Dan said, lifting her chin with a finger to get a better look at her face.

Her eyes were still drenched with tears, but she looked just as fierce as she had in the parking lot. "No one gets to do that. No one gets to hurt my patients."

"I know. I know." He hugged her again, making the cat protest. "Hell of a swing, darling. Really."

Jake came back in. "Your lock's been

jimmied and your alarm's wires have been cut."

"Why?" Dan could tell that Adele was still half-pissed, but now it was tendered with a dollop of bafflement.

Jake leaned on the wall. "Guy had on gloves. There won't be prints in here, but since you both saw him coming out, and he's got some fierce cat scratches, I'm thinking we won't have to worry about prints when you press charges. We'll see if he'll tell us something, but I bet this is about that dog."

"Which dog?" She had the answer before anyone could answer. "Oh. Hatter."

"Exactly. All the other dogs are locally owned, right?"

She glanced along the kennels. "Yes. They are."

"Someone knows he's here then." Jake's scowl was black. "There's a leak. Either it's in my shop, or it's in Suarez or Emerson's offices. I'll let them know."

"I'm taking him home," Adele declared suddenly. "I'm putting a damn sign on the door to say he's gone and not to bust into my clinic."

"That's a start," Jake said, still frowning. "What if they come to your house?"

"My two dogs, three with Hatter, are big,

noisy and loose. There's a big-ass fence and you need a code to get in the gate." She set Ribald down with a long stroke to his back, much to the cat's annoyance. She let Dan help her up. "No way anyone's getting into my place to get him."

"As if Hatter, or your two, would let anyone in," Jake said, nodding. "Yeah. I get that. A good solution for tonight. One of my guys will take a swing by here every hour as they patrol, just to be sure."

"Thank you."

Jake nodded and pushed off the wall. "I'll go in and see if our burglar has lawyered up or if he's in a mood to chat. Talk to you tomorrow."

"Sounds good," Adele said, and Dan agreed.

Jake left, and Adele put things to rights, standing up bins and putting things back onto the counters where they'd been knocked off.

When she was done, and seemed to be aimlessly straightening things instead of actually doing anything new, Dan stopped her.

"Let's head to your house. You can run me home later or I'll call Vince at the TaxiHaus and get a ride back to my car."

"Good." She nodded. "Okay. Thanks." He wasn't fooled at all by her acquiescence.

She was obviously tired and thinking about Hatter and the missing little girl.

To his surprise, after she'd locked up the clinic as best she could, she led Hatter to the passenger side of the truck and helped him in. She handed Dan the keys.

"Do you mind?" she said, gesturing to the driver's side.

"Not at all."

Hatter sat up, happy and proud in the middle of the seat as Dan got in. Without another word, he turned the truck toward Adele's house.

They pulled up to the gates of her two-acre property and she gave him the code for the gate. He pulled in and, as he crossed the cattle guard, he felt the tingle of magick.

"You have wards?"

"Of course," she said matter of factly. "I can't use them at the clinic. Too many people coming and going, too many employees and so on. I have general spells there, for healing and energy work, but here, I can ward to my heart's content."

He smiled at that, and drove down the well-maintained gravel drive. Hatter perked up as Adele's dogs barked, heralding their arrival.

Adele helped the big dog down from the

truck. "Come on in," she said, holding out a hand for Dan.

He took it and together they walked into her neatly renovated, but very old, farmhouse. The kitchen was immaculate, and Adele's two dogs bustled around Hatter and Dan in equal curiosity.

"Hercules is the Boxer, and Patronus is the white husky-looking beast currently play-bowing to Hatter," she explained. "C'mon guys," she said to the dogs. "Take it outside." She let them out into the well-lit backyard. After watching them for a moment, she turned back into the kitchen. "Would you like a beer or a glass of wine?"

"Beer would be good," he said. "It's been a hell of a night."

"It has." As he watched she pulled two beers out of the fridge, popped the caps and held one out. She didn't look as fierce or mad as she had at the clinic. Now, she just looked worried, and weary.

"Hey," he said, setting the beer on the counter. "You look like you could use this." He drew her into his arms and just held her. To his delight, after a moment she relaxed into his embrace and put her cheek on his chest.

"Thanks," she said, her voice muffled

against his shirt. "You're right. I needed a hug."

He kissed the top of her head. She was a lot shorter than he was, which always surprised him. Her personality was so bright and vibrant, it wasn't until she was like this that he realized how vulnerable and petite she was. The glints of red in her hair shone more prominently in the bright glare of the overhead light. He'd noticed them before, but they seemed jewel-like and beautiful now. He pressed another kiss to her hair, snugging her closer.

His body had the inevitable reaction, but he wasn't going to do anything about it. She didn't need any pressure from him right now.

But when she turned her face up to his, he had to kiss her. She wasn't classically beautiful. Nor was she model-pretty. But she had a glow from within that did something for him. It turned him on physically, sure, but it did something to his gut, to his heart, that he couldn't categorize.

"What is it?" she said, staring at him.

"Just thinking how much I like looking at you," he admitted.

Her lips curved. "I'm pretty fond of looking at you too. You have really great lips, did you know that?" She raised a hand and traced the curve of his upper lip. The touch hit him low and hard in his gut. Everything within him came to attention, emotionally and physically at the feather-light caress.

"I like your lips too." He bent down to brush his lips over hers. A tease of a kiss.

Adele's hands dove into his hair—something he'd discovered really turned him on—and pulled his head back to hers.

"Kiss me again, like you mean it."

"Happy to oblige," he said. With that permission, he dove in, his mouth fused to hers, their tongues in a mad dance of passion, the kiss fanning the flames of his need.

The kitchen bar stool bumped him in the back, appearing as if by magick, and he sat. Adele stepped in between his legs this time, reversing what they'd done at the clinic. He pulled her closer. Neither one of them were hiding their desire now.

He quit thinking of magick, or the dogs, or the kitchen as Adele settled into him, her hands running up his bare back under his shirt. Her touch made him impossibly harder, needier.

He never wanted to take advantage of an emotional moment, do something she'd regret. If he had to stop, and go home, he needed to do it now.

"Adele," he said, breaking the kiss and easing back just a fraction. His hands were on her back as well. He didn't realize he'd copied her move, sliding her shirt out of her pants to caress the soft skin at her side. He'd felt the ridge of a scar along her ribs, and his fingers rested there as he tried to gain a measure of composure.

"Hmmmm?" she made the questioning noise against his neck where she was nibbling her way along the pulse.

"I don't want to take advantage." He framed her face with his hands, pulling her from the intensely pleasurable path she was making along his collarbone. He punctuated his words with kisses to her eyes, her nose, her cheeks and her lips. "I also don't want to rush you or push you. I'm interested in more than this."

"You're not interested in sex?"

He laughed and kissed her again. "You're driving me mad with wanting you."

"But?" She pulled back a bit, looking into his eyes.

"It's been a crazy night. I don't want you to think—"

She shook her head. "I don't."

"Okay." Now he let her see the need, the desire. But he also gave her the words, as he tucked a tendril of her silky hair behind her ear. "I've wanted you for a long time."

"Will you stay?"

CHAPTER FOUR

For Adele, it was a loaded question. Dan didn't look away or prevaricate or offer some off-the-cuff remark.

He met her gaze and she saw the desire. It matched her own and, seeing it, she nearly melted. He really wanted her as badly as she wanted him.

Thank the Gods the feeling was mutual.

"If you're sure," Dan said, "then yes."

"I'm sure."

No sooner were the words out of her mouth than Dan kissed her again. His mouth claimed hers and he pulled her in again. When that wasn't close enough, he stood, still kissing her, and lifted her onto the kitchen counter. That put them on a level, and turned her on so much she nearly orgasmed right then and there at the strength and power of him.

He made a noise of approval when she was on the same level and he could kiss her even more deeply.

"This needs to come off," he said between kisses, pushing at her soft sweater. She'd worn it for the Coven meeting, hoping he'd notice. She'd also worn a lacey confection of a bra underneath it. It made her feel feminine to wear great underwear under her habitual, utilitarian scrubs and professional white coat, so she always had nice bras.

This one, however, was meant to inflame the senses. When she pulled her sweater off, it apparently did its job.

"Oh, yeah," he groaned, his hands shaping her breasts over the lacy cups. "I'm glad I didn't know you were wearing this."

"Why?"

"I'd have had to drag you out into the parking lot to neck in a dark corner."

"I thought about you when I put it on tonight," she admitted. "I thought about what you'd think if you saw it."

"I think it's fabulous. I think you're amazing. This," he flicked the hooks undone, "is icing on a very delicious cake." He slid the confection down her arms and she felt a brush of vulnerability. Then Dan slid his hands up her rib cage to cup her breasts and every other thought flew out of her head. Even when his hands hesitated over the scar, she just enjoyed. This time, she refused to be distracted by the past.

"Oh my," she moaned as his big hand closed over her breast. She let her head fall back and let her body surrender to the strength of the arm he banded around her waist. "You have the best hands. I noticed your hands the first time we met."

"Really?" Dan bent to run kisses up the amazing line of her neck, since she'd presented it so nicely when she moaned. Her nipple was a taut bud against his palm and he pressed in, and then ghosted his palm over its peak, drawing another moan from Adele. She was so responsive, so beautiful. His erection strained the confines of his khakis, he tried to ignore it as he turned his attention to her other breast.

"I want to touch you," she said, sitting up, tugging at his shirt. He obliged her, pulling it off over his head when she'd unbuttoned it enough for him to do so. He pulled off the plain white t-shirt underneath and nearly came at the look on her face and the touch of her hands.

When she leaned into him, pressing kisses to his chest, he closed his eyes and clenched his body. Everything about her made him want her, his cock throbbed in time with her kisses, and the caveman part of his brain wanted to tear off her pants and thrust immediately into her wet heat.

"What are you thinking?" she asked.

"How much I want you."

"Mmm," she made the sound sultry and inviting and he pulled her to the edge of the counter. It was the perfect height for making a feast of her.

"Will you let me taste you?" he asked, praying she'd say yes.

Her eyes widened and he unsnapped her jeans, tugged down the zipper. When she wiggled a little, he took that as encouragement. She kicked off her shoes and braced herself on her arms, which let him tug the jeans off her hips and over her beautiful thighs. The pants and her panties pooled on the floor as he feasted his eyes on her gorgeous form.

"You're perfectly made, do you know that?" He ran his hands down her sides, and over her legs. She'd brought her knees together as he divested her of her pants, but he wanted to see her. "I want to taste you, to make you scream with pleasure."

When she hesitated, he said, "Do you like to be kissed there?" When she nodded, he added, "Then let me make you feel good."

He pressed a kiss just above her knee, sliding his hand over the other creamy thigh. She let her legs part and he just about died at the sight of her femininity, every inch of her beautifully made.

"Okay," she said, her voice a husky rasp that drew him in to kiss her again. He caressed her hip and the curve of her backside.

"So beautiful." He bent to kiss her breasts again. As she had before, she let her head fall back exposing her neck. She was in his blood now, his heartbeat pounding with desire for her. He licked and kissed his way down her taut belly, letting his hands warm her legs as he eased down to kiss her inner thighs. "I want you to feel good."

"Promises, promises," she rasped, as her breath quickened. "Don't stop."

"I won't."

He gently pushed at her shoulders, encouraging her to lie back on the granite of the kitchen island. When she did, he brought her hands to his mouth and kissed them. His gaze locked with hers, he slid his hands up her arms and over her shoulders, the lightest of touches. Then he skimmed his palms down over her breasts and belly, and back to her thighs, which he nudged open just a little more. She was a feast to be savored, but he didn't think he could wait any longer.

He pressed kisses along the jut of her hip and she slid her fingers into his hair. When he moved lower, stroking his fingers into her curls, coming nearer and nearer to the wet slickness that beckoned him, she moved restlessly on the counter.

Smiling, he paused, and waited until she opened her eyes. She lifted her head and looked at him. "Dan?"

He stroked a finger slowly through her wet folds and she gasped, letting her head drop back once more. "Adele," he said, her name a caress as he stroked through again and again, lightly caressing her clitoris each time. That had her arching off the counter. His cock jerked, straining to be free. It was all he could do to ignore it, and keep it slow, keep it about her.

"Do you like this?" he said, sliding his finger toward the entrance of her body, teasing around the edges, then penetrating just a bit. She gripped his hair and gasped as he dipped in and out. That drew more gasps and made her even wetter.

"I love it. More," she demanded, and he slid his finger all the way in, sliding it out, then making it two fingers so that he could feel her muscles clenching on him. When he bent to run his tongue over the same path his fingers had taken, she came with a rush. He back arched and she uttered a half-scream of pleasure. He drew out the pulsing orgasm as long as he could, moving his fingers and his mouth until she sank back against the countertop.

She rolled her hips against his hand and it was his turn to moan. Gods, he was about to die with the need to take, but he bore down. He wanted her pleasure first.

"Dan, please," she said, looking at him, heavy lidded and satisfied. "I want you inside me. I need to feel you."

Thank every little God ever named.

It was all he could think as he helped her off the counter. Her knees were wobbly and he felt a thrill of pride that he'd brought her such release. When she reached for him, slid her hand over his arousal, he hissed in the pleasure-pain of contact.

"If you do much of that, I'll embarrass myself."

"Then come in here, and come in me," she

said, a siren clothed in only a sultry smile as she led him into the sitting room. She pushed down his pants, and then pushed him onto the couch. "I need to pleasure you, too."

He gripped her hands before she could touch him again. "Adele, I'm serious, I won't last if you touch me."

"What if I lick you?"

He groaned and nearly came at the thought. He forced himself to think about the Dewey Decimal System. And filing. And mending book spines.

"No licking," he said through gritted teeth. "Not yet. And we need protection. It's in my pocket."

"I'm glad you're prepared," she murmured, dropping to her knees to fish the condom out of his pocket. The sight of her, kneeling in front of him, her hair all silky and gorgeous, was one of the most glorious things he'd ever seen. "How about I put this on you?" She suited actions to words and had the condom on him without him exploding, but it was a near thing.

"Come here," he demanded, pulling her up onto the couch. "Do you want to ride?

"Oh, my yes," she murmured, positioning herself over him, with her legs on either side of his. "I'm so ready for this. I've wanted you for ages," she declared, looking into his eyes.

She pressed her mouth to his as she took him in, sliding down onto him ever so slowly. His eyes threatened to roll back in his head as her inner muscles squeezed him when she took him to the hilt.

"Oh, you feel so good," she murmured, when she'd taken him in. "You're stretching me to the limit and oh, hell, I'm going to come, just..." And she did, clenching around him so tightly that he had to grip her hips and hold her still so that he didn't completely lose control.

It was a pleasurable, agonizing eternity before she rose slightly then came back down on him, sliding her breasts against his chest in a friction designed to drive him mad. The caress of her body on his enflamed him.

"I want to flip you over and drive into you," he said, his voice a growl as he struggled to maintain.

"Do it," she urged. "I want you to."

"You sure?"

"Yes."

He lifted her as he stood, barely breaking their intimate contact as they shifted positions.

She wrapped an arm around his neck,

pulling him down for a kiss. With the other hand, she pulled his hip, driving him in so deeply that they both gasped.

He pulled out, slowly, drawing out the pleasure, before sliding back in just as slowly. And again.

"You're teasing me," she said, arching her back so that her hips rose and rolled against him, driving him deeper. "I want you."

Her words snapped the leash this time. Knowing she wanted him as he wanted her, having her say it, be there, and be so wet and hot and beautiful. He thrust in and she moaned, and rose to meet him every time until they were panting and gripping one another with ferocious desire.

He felt the build and with one last thrust of his hips, his back locked and he came in a wild rush. Adele cried out and her body clenched around him as she, too, orgasmed.

His breath came in harsh gasps as he felt the internal aftershocks of her pleasure. He struggled to recover, to reorder his scattered thoughts.

"Bright Lady," she rasped. "You…"

She stopped talking to swallow.

"I?"

"Are magnificent." She stroked along his side, down over his hip to his backside, pulling him in again, which made pleasure ripple along his spine once more.

"I'd say the same, if I could talk," he rasped.

She smiled. "Water."

"Absolutely," he managed. "As soon as I regain the ability for independent movement."

She laughed. "Now I'm hungry again."

"Water. Food. Yes," he said, and laughed with her.

They lay together, each catching their breath. They kissed and touched again and again as they cleaned up and he pulled on his jeans. She went to let the dogs back in. "I didn't mean to leave them outside," she said, ruffling Hatter's ears carefully.

"They seem to be okay with it," he said.

"Yeah, but it's not very professional of me to have left a client's dog outside for..." she looked at her kitchen clock and her eyes widened. "Wow. Nearly an hour. Especially when someone was after him."

"They've been fed, they had water, they played. And your gate alarm and the dogs themselves would have told us if someone was around, right?" He stood behind her, pulled her into his arms, back to front. Her clothes were all in the kitchen, so she was still gloriously naked.

"Yes." She said, rubbing her back against him. "You're right."

"Then it's all good. I won't tell," he whispered in her ear. "By the way, did I tell you I think you're amazing?"

Adele snuggled in. "You are too."

He kissed her neck. "Do you want me to go?"

She laughed and turned into his arms. "Are you crazy?"

CHAPTER FIVE

"Define crazy," he said, and she laughed.

Now would be the perfect time to tell her about his ghosts. He wasn't crazy, but some things about his life were crazy.

"Wasn't it you telling me that everyone in Haven Harbor is crazy?" she said, drawing his head down for a kiss.

"True," he admitted. "But I've got some pretty odd things in my skeleton closet," he began, just as the dogs alerted and started barking. There was a noise on the porch. It sounded like the whoosh of water, but he knew that couldn't be.

"The gate didn't alarm," he said, moving in front of her. Shit! She was naked and he was only half-dressed. Not the way to confront bad guys. "Get my phone and call Jake."

"Owls," she said, laughing. She dashed to the kitchen island and pulled her sweater on, then slipped into her jeans and shoes.

"What?"

"Owls," she repeated. "I can't believe they've come back." She tugged on his hand. "You want crazy? Come see my owls."

She grabbed her coat off the peg just inside the door and stepped outside. He followed her out and very nearly gaped. Having grown up in Haven Harbor, and now, being the Coven record keeper, he'd seen and read about some amazing things. This, however, was new. There were at least fifteen owls in the trees near the house and on the roof of the garage. It looked like a scene from a Harry Potter movie.

"Seriously?"

"Did you know that they call a group of owls a Parliament?"

Dan laughed, and shivered in the cold. He didn't want to go it though, still amazed at what he was seeing. "Actually, I did know that."

"Right. Librarian." She smiled up at him. "You know cool stuff. That's impressed me from day one."

The words warmed him, but he was still

distracted by the feathered guests. "So, why is there a parliament of owls in your garden?"

"One of the witches who built this house, sometime in the seventeen-fifties, hand raised some owls that had fallen from the nest. They came back and nested, and so on, and so on. Every so often a bunch of them have a group chat in the backyard."

"And you chat with them?" he said, smiling. "What witch wouldn't?"

"Exactly. I've helped a few of them too," she said, reaching into the house and pulling out a coat for him. "Here, put this on, it's my dad's. He's always leaving stuff here."

"How've you helped them?" He shrugged into the coat, which, amazingly, fit him.

"A broken wing once. That owl let me set the wing, and took mice from me for a few weeks until it healed. When I unsplinted the wing, it managed its own recovery from there." She paused, then added, "I think these are some pretty smart owls. Maybe that long-ago witch used magick around them. Maybe it affected them. I don't know, but they don't act like regular, wild owls. They're different."

She was watching him, he realized, to see how he took this news of something different about her.

No worries there. If anyone's different, it's me. Hell, bloodline ghosts come to visit me all the time, that's definitely different.

"Everyone's got a quirk, right?" he said, ready to tell her. Before he could say anything else, an enormous great horned owl swooped right onto the porch. It landed on one foot on the porch railing, backwinging furiously to keep its balance. The other foot was held up, close to the owl's body. When the bird settled, Dan could see the foot was pierced through with a piece of painted wood.

"Bloody hell," she said, moving forward. "That's a piece of an arrow."

Dan started to pull her back, but realized what he was about to do and stopped. Jake was right. He was a moron if he thought he could change her or wrap her up in bubble wrap for her own protection.

She glanced at him. "They haven't hurt me yet."

"I get it," he said, watching every move the owl made. The owl was watching Dan with equal intensity, swiveling his head, then bobbing it up and down. It would have been comical had the owl not been hissing and clacking it's very sharp predator's beak at the same time. It was patently obvious that it was warning Dan, not Adele.

"Would you go into the kitchen for me?" Adele asked, not taking her eyes off the bird now. "I need gloves, gauze squares, tape and some antibiotic ointment. They're in my emergency bag, just inside the door."

"Got it." Dan backed up slowly, and went inside, hurrying to grab what she needed.

When he came back out, she was on one knee, at eye level with the owl's wounded foot.

"Normally, no sane person would ever attempt something like this," she said conversationally, without turning to look at him. "If Dolores Webb hadn't told me the story about the first witch and the owls when I bought the house, I wouldn't have even come outside when they first showed up."

"When was that?"

"Three years ago when I moved in and bought Dr. Gerrish's practice."

"I came back the next year." He'd heard the gossip about the new vet, and how pretty she was.

"Yeah." She held out a hand for the gloves. She still didn't look at him. "Okay, Mr. Prime Minister," she said to the owl. "Let's do this."

Adele pulled on the gloves, opened a gauze pad and held out her hand. To his surprise, the owl gingerly set his sharply-taloned foot into her hand. She nodded. The owl nodded.

She bent her head and looked at the wound. From what he could see, the splintered piece of the arrow was caught in the webbing between the owl's toes. Had it just been in one part of the webbing, the creature might have pulled it out himself. But it spanned two parts of the webbing, binding the toes into an unnatural bunch.

"I think if I can get this out, and put antibiotic on it, it'll heal just fine."

"How can I help?" He wanted to snatch her to safety, but he knew better.

"Go down in the yard and get a stick for him to bite on."

"Seriously?" Dan was shocked out of his worry by her request.

"I'd rather he bit a stick than me."

"Good point," Dan agreed as he trotted down the steps. His breath steamed in the chill October air.

Not far into the garden he picked up a good sized stick, and broke it into a manageable size. Owls watched him from perches all over the yard. The majority of them were smaller Great Horned Owls. But he caught sight of several barn owls, and maybe a screech owl, but he couldn't be sure.

As he turned back to the house, he grinned. All Adele's Halloween decorations had lighted up, probably on timers. Between that and the owls it was a scene from an old-timey Halloween print.

When he offered the stick, the bird just looked at him, then at Adele. She stared at the creature and it turned and nipped the stick out of his hand with lightning speed. It seemed to chuckle a little at his startlement.

"Okay, here goes nothing," she said, and, having moistened the whole foot with antibiotic ointment, she pulled the splintered wood free. With a crack like a bullet, the owl snapped the branch it held, the pieces clattering onto the porch floor like spent shotgun shells.

Adele pressed two more gauze pads to the wound, waiting for it to clot. When it finally did, she put more ointment on the area, spreading the gel around to all surfaces of the foot anywhere near the wound.

The bird watched her with keen intensity, lifting the foot and setting it back down as if to prove that it was finally functioning again now that the long splinter was removed.

"There you go," she said, after putting on a carefully placed dressing. She stood up slowly and moved back. "Come back tomorrow and

I'll put more ointment on it." She held up the tube.

"Do you think he understands?"

"I have no idea if he or she gets it," Adele said, giving the owl plenty of room. "But I'd bet cold cash that its back here tomorrow."

"I want to see that," he said.

"After dinner, you can come back," she said, then stopped. "If you want to, that is."

Together they moved further back and the owl, half rousing his wings, shook all over, then took off into the trees. Other than the first snap of his wings, he was silent as the wind. The others took off in twos and threes, just as quietly, until the whole clearing was empty once more.

"If I hadn't just seen that, I wouldn't have believed it."

"A Haven Harbor moment," she said. She stepped away from him. "So?"

"So what?"

"It's weird. I talk to animals."

"Like I said, we've all got our own weird."

"You should put that on a t-shirt." She moved past him when he opened the door for her.

He grinned. "Maybe I will. Can you see Sam in a shirt with that on it? Priceless."

She laughed and said, "Hey, Dan, Dan, the

Librarian Man?"

Surprised at the rhyme, he stopped, staring at her. "Yes?"

"What do you say we go to bed?"

His smile stretched until he felt the ache of it in his cheeks.

"I say yes, ma'am, Dr. Picard."

CHAPTER SIX

They woke at dawn, despite having gotten to bed late. Sometime during the night, Adele had turned and spooned into him. He woke with his hand curved over her breast and his body primed for her.

"Mmmmff," she muttered, shifting her backside so that it rubbed his rock-hard erection. They'd made love again right after they'd gotten in bed. She'd pulled on a flannel nightie, and he'd had his boxers on. Those ended up right back on the floor. They'd snickered at the put-the-clothes-on-take-the-clothes-off adventures in the bedroom.

After that second bout of lovemaking, however, they'd talked until they drifted off to sleep, held tightly in one another's arms.

Now, with her warm and soft under his hands, he stroked her, rousing her slowly, and gently. He slid his hand up along her hip, stroking her smooth skin. She opened for him, so that his next stroke up brought his hand up the front of her thigh. Since she'd been so obliging as to shift positions, he cupped the wet heat of her, parting the curls at the apex of her thighs with a gentle finger.

"Just feeling you stroke me has me wet," she whispered.

"I love your skin," he said, pressing a kiss to her shoulder. "So soft and smooth."

"Mmmm." She raised a hand, pulling his head down for a kiss. "You feel good to me too," she purred the words as she kissed him, long and deep. "Come here." Sliding over, she pulled him on top, spreading her legs to accommodate his bigger body. "Come here, Dan."

"Your wish is my command," he said, letting her guide him in, shuddering at the intimacy of that act, of her acceptance of him.

"Wow," she murmured as she closed her eyes again. "Better than I remembered," she said as she took every inch of him. When he moved, she shifted her hips to meet him.

Her eyes popped open and she smiled. "You are formidable, Dan Nutter, but I can take you."

Dan laughed, and flexed his hips. She shuddered. "You just like to see me come," she protested.

"Yes, I do." He flexed again. "Are you going to?"

"I am," she admitted and so he pulled out and thrust back in, tantalizing her, bringing her to the edge. "Now," she demanded. "Harder."

He obliged and saw actual stars when their coupling brought him to the brink of orgasm, then pushed him over into a kaleidoscope of color and pleasure as they climaxed together.

When they stopped breathing like sprinters and their heartrates calmed, she said, "We're getting better at that."

"Practice," he rasped, his throat dry again. "Makes perfect."

She stroked down his back. "Too true."

####

Adele didn't know what to make of herself this morning. She'd been smiling since she left the house.

She'd woken with Dan, they'd made mind-blowing love in the pre-dawn hours, then slept for another forty-five minutes and repeated the trick in the shower. She was pretty sure she was walking funny, but since she'd been working in her office since her staff arrived, no one had noticed.

Hatter lay on a dog bed behind her desk on the blanket Thomas Spradling had couriered to her. Hercules and Patronus were on matching beds in front of the desk. A plastic doggy gate blocked the door. She wasn't letting anyone stay alone today.

She'd driven Dan back to his car before seven so he could get home and change for work. They'd very nearly ended up in the backseat when he'd kissed her good-bye.

Damn, the man could kiss!

Adele couldn't believe they'd finally gotten together. The heat between them had been obvious to everyone, but Adele hadn't wanted to make the first move. Evidently, Dan had been hesitant too. But whatever errand had him out on the road to help her the other night, she was grateful. Not only had she saved Hatter, but she and Dan had managed to start a thing.

"No idea what the *thing* is," she muttered to herself as she filled out charts and finished paperwork. "But it's definitely a thing."

She stacked up another folder on the finished charts and began reading and filling in an order form. She signed it with a flourish and had just pulled down the next batch of files when Darlene appeared in the doorway.

"Agent Suarez is here to see you," she said.

"Give me five, then bring him back."

"Got it."

Adele grabbed her phone and texted both Dan and Jake. They'd both wanted to be notified if either Emerson or Suarez contacted her about Hatter. She then took the three dogs into the enclosed area behind the clinic. The large outdoor exercise area was covered, which was good, since it was drizzling. The dogs would be safe and comfortable, despite the rain and the cool temps, while she talked to Suarez.

"Agent," she said when he came in and sat down. "How can I help you?"

"I'm not sure, Dr. Picard. We've had a few breaks in the case, some new leads which I'm not at liberty to discuss," he said, forestalling her question. "However, you may be able to help us. Do you know anything about bats?"

"Bats?" That was a question out of left field. "A little, why?"

"We found traces of bat droppings on Dr. Spradling's driveway where the kidnappers supposedly parked. There was also a type of sand or soil that's found mostly here in Haven County and counties north of here, toward the state line, according to the lab. Since Dr.

Spradling's never been up here, its October and I'm told its too cold for bats in Boston at this point, it makes a connection to Haven Harbor. So we're hoping you might know where, around here, there might be bats."

She pondered that. "This is so not my area of expertise. You'd want Trudi McIntyre, who's a naturalist. Maybe Lydia Webb, who collects herbs and plants all through the woods and swamps around Haven. I don't know if you've considered it, but there are a number of reputable psychics in town who might be able to help locate Thomas's daughter. Especially if she's anywhere near here."

Maybe this was why she was supposed to have Hatter! If the girl was here...

Suarez frowned, shook his head in the negative. "I'm quite sure they're nice people." She must have looked puzzled because he added, "the psychics. However, I've got to keep this close. We're closing in, thanks to you finding Hatter."

"I'm glad. And I get it." She hope, if they didn't find Gabrielle soon, that Thomas would agree to getting Dolores Webb to dowse, or having Madame Sabina see what she could See. She couldn't do it without his permission, but... "I'll ask around about the bats. I can ask and not draw attention to it."

"Exactly. Thank you. If your Chief Strongbow asks, people will be curious. If you ask, as an animal expert, people won't bat an eye, so to speak." His lips quirked a bit at the unintended pun. "How's the dog?"

"He's healing well. Do you want me to release him to Dr. Spradling?"

"Not yet. The good doctor isn't ready for the dog, in my opinion. He's overwrought. The little girl is well-loved, and with Dr. Spradling's wife dying when Gabrielle was only four, Gabrielle is all he has."

Tears pricked her eyes. How terrible for Thomas to have lost his wife, and now, his daughter was missing.

"I'll find out about the bats," she assured him. "Please let me know if there's anything else I can help with."

"I will." Suarez asked a few more questions, then took his leave. She considered everything he'd asked as she brought the three big dogs back into her office. They each settled down with a bit of jostling as she handed chew-bones to each of them.

Bats? How did she find out about bats?

The answer was so simple, she made a disgusted sound. "Idiot. Call the library.

And the ever-so-sexy librarian."

She did just that.

"Hey." It was all he said when he answered, but his voice was low, husky and intimate. Just for her, the tone said. Only for her.

It warmed her to her toes.

"Hey," she echoed his word. "I need some help."

"Anything."

"Bats," she said, laughing when she felt his shocked silence. "Seriously. I'm making a serious request of my town librarian. I need to know about bats in Haven County. Suarez stopped by."

"I got your text," he replied. "He didn't stay long?"

"Just long enough to ask if I knew anything about bats and where they might hang out in Haven County. Seems some of their tests indicated the getaway car had bat guano on its tires."

"Well that should be an interesting search set," he said, and she heard keys clicking in the background. "What else are you doing today?"

"Mostly office stuff. I don't have clinic hours on Friday till afternoon."

"We still on for tonight?"

Everything within her leapt up. Now that they'd slept together, he could have assumed he didn't have to take her out, that they could just stay in.

"I'm looking forward to it. I'm going to head out of here around five, take the dogs home and feed them, then get ready. Will you pick me up?"

"Of course," he said, like that was a foregone conclusion. "I'll get back to you on the bats in a little bit."

"Okay."

With a smile, she prepared to deal with her patient load for the afternoon.

####

At the stroke of five, she hustled the last of her chatty patients out of the door and locked it.

"Darlene, are you and Jessica okay to lock up?"

"Of course," Darlene said, looking up from the data she was entering into the computer. "The alarm's been rewired and reset today, the new lock went in. We're right and tight"

"Excellent. I'm out of here."

"Have a great date."

Adele just waved and left with the three dogs on her heels. Of course everyone knew she had a date with Dan. The gossip trees in

Haven Harbor were as well-manned as the emergency contact trees. It was pretty hard to hide anything in a town this small.

She piled the dogs in the truck and looked at the data Dan had sent her.

Dan: The only major note I found about bat populations in Haven County is about seventy-five years old. It says that there was an enormous bat colony in a sea cave, but that they were dispersed after a spring cave-in opened the sheltered interior space to the elements. There's another reference from back in the nineteen-eighties about some bats in an abandoned house up north of you, the Gilman place, but nothing else. Helpful?

Adele: No idea! She sent, and added an emoji. *Dolores showed me the Gilman place when I was buying. I remember where it is, so I'm going to drive up there before I head home, just to see it. It's not far from my place.*

Dan: Be careful.

Adele: Will do.

It warmed her, on one hand, that he was worried about her. When you lived alone and no one really knew if you came or went on time, or even if you made it home at night, it was comforting to have someone who cared.

On the other hand, she could take it as an implication that he thought she didn't know what she was doing.

"Which would suck," she told the dogs. "But I'm going to be positive. He cares, and it's nice."

Hatter licked her cheek. "I know, right? I like that someone cares. I just want him to see me as confident and competent, too."

She drove up past the mill and bakery, and took the left fork down Amesbury road, which ran past her place, and, if memory served, ran past the old Gilman place as well. It had been built even earlier than Adele's own house. The Gilman place was, in fact, one of the first outlying farms to have been built in Haven Harbor.

She passed the drive for it, and had to back up to peer down the way. The remains of a rusty fence and chain lay broken in the dusty driveway. She could see that trees lined the drive and went three and four deep on the left side. The broad, low trees were full of ripening apples. The house sat on a rise, so most of it was above the trees. The roof was intact, though it had been patched in places, and the paint was peeling. The windows were boarded up and the shutters were hanging down at crazy angles.

There was no sign of life, no Halloween décor, nothing to show anyone lived there. No cars. The grass was mowed. But it felt deserted.

She rolled down the window, instead of peering through the dog-spooged window glass. Hatter whined, pushing into her lap to sniff the wind. The other two dogs stood to peer out and enjoy the fresh air when she opened the other window, but Hatter stood on her lap, shoving his head out her window to catch the wind.

"Should I go in there?" she wondered aloud. She should leave it to the Sheriff. Or Chief Strongbow. Or Suarez and Emerson.

Hatter whined again, but she didn't want to chance anything.

"Okay, okay," she said to the dogs, doing a u-turn in the road. "I'll be smart about this. Besides, not only do I have anything to report, but I've got to get ready for my date."

She thought about the house all the way home, though. There was something about it that bothered her. Nothing obvious, just a weird feeling. It wasn't the lack of decoration, although for Haven Harbor at Halloween, the undecorated house was definitely an anomaly.

By the time Dan picked her up, she'd shaken off the feeling of unease and was ready to go out and enjoy herself with a fascinating man who was rapidly becoming more and more important to her.

They had a lovely dinner at The Judges Chambers, one of the nicest restaurants in town. By the time they were headed home, they'd been flirting for two hours and she was ready to jump his bones.

This time, they stumbled into the house, laughing as they kissed and stripped on the way in. They paused only long enough to let the dogs out and then in again, leaving them in the kitchen.

"This time I want a bed for the main event," she said, tugging him up the stairs with her. She pulled at his suit jacket and he let it slide off his shoulders to puddle on the floor. He unzipped her skirt as they kissed and she wiggled her hips and it too dropped. She kicked off her shoes and he managed to get his off as well.

He laughed as she dashed into the bedroom. He followed.

They made love with laughter, fumbling with clothes and the condom. They laughed over everything until Adele was dizzy with the fun of it. The only serious moment was when they connected in the most sensual way.

"Ohhhhhh," Adele gasped. "How is it possible for this to feel even better?"

"I don't know, but I'm so glad."

"I am too," she purred. "It's been a while."

Somehow the admission made him feel ten feet tall. She'd waited for him.

"Now, Dan, now," she gasped, rising to meet his thrusts and pulling him closer, deeper, harder.

"Oh, my Gods," he growled, as he felt the build of orgasm. "Adele!"

They came together and he stopped breathing as his body convulsed in pleasure. He wheezed as he recovered. "By the Lady, Adele," he managed as he collapsed, bracing on his elbows so he didn't crush her. "You make me crazy."

"Me?" she managed, as she too tried to regain some composure. "You're the one who told me at dinner that you wanted to bite my neck and lick my breasts."

"I did do that, didn't I?" He smiled smugly.

"You did," she mock-accused. "And you told me you'd like to—"

"Yes?" he inquired, as he pressed his face into her neck, licking and kissing her as she squirmed. "Tastes great."

They played a while longer, but thirst drove them to get untangled and clean up, then headed to the kitchen. "You take my breath away so often I'm going to need to keep water on the bedside table."

He was barefoot, and had pulled on his suit pants and zipped them so they'd stay on. She was wearing his shirt and nothing else.

The dogs swirled around them as she made stood in the door of the open refrigerator. She offered him wine or beer, but she looked so adorable he had to go kiss her.

"I don't know, water first, then maybe a beer," he said. She was kissing him when the dogs alerted, facing the dining room.

"What?" In a flash, she opened the drawer next to the fridge. She pulled out a long knife, longer than he'd ever seen. He moved in front of her, trying to see what had riled the dogs up. She moved around him.

"Jeez, Adele, first a baseball bat, now a knife the size of a Texas chainsaw?"

"You have a better idea?"

He felt the frigid draft that preceded a visitation. "Shit."

"What?"

He moved to flank her again. "I know what this is."

"What?" her voice was steady, but he heard the underlying thread of concern.

Hatter growled and Hercules and Patronus followed suit. Patronus, however, ducked behind Adele's knees. The dog was huge, but instead of jumping to the fore like Hatter and

Hercules, he was behind Adele.

"So, this is where I find you," a chill, male voice spoke into the silence. A misty form floated in the air. The ghost became clearer as the moments passed.

"Stay behind me," Dan said. "What do you want Grampa Pritchard?"

"You know him?" Adele hissed.

"I do," Dan said, his heart sinking at her shocked tone. "You're interrupting. What do you want?"

"I'm interested in the dog. I see you have it here. I can help you with what he needs to do."

"Which dog?"

"That one." The ghost pointed at Hatter who was still growling, his fur on his back standing on end, and his head down in attack mode.

"Dan, what the hell is going on?" Adele demanded.

"My family likes to hang around as ghosts. They come and talk to me."

"Oh, you didn't tell her about our *family curse?*" the ghost moaned the words.

"Don't be so dramatic, Grampa. It's not a curse," Dan said, disgusted with his ancestor and furious with himself that he'd not told Adele before one of his ancestors sprung his

Gift on her.

"Speak for yourself boy," the ghost intoned. "Staying here, tied to you, can be a curse."

Irritated as hell, and now afraid, Dan snarled. "Get out, Grandpa. I've got things to do."

The ghost harrumphed, and disappeared.

He pivoted and faced Adele. "It's not what it seems."

"You didn't tell me about this…this…thing you've got." She waved toward where the ghost had appeared. "I told you about my weird and you didn't think to mention *this?* This is major."

"You didn't tell me about the whammy you have with the dogs until you had to. And the owls." He cursed inside. He sounded defensive, dammit. That was the wrong way to handle this, but he could see the whole situation spiraling down the drain.

"It didn't come up," she snapped. "We weren't spending a lot of time talking."

"I know," he said, reaching for her, trying to bring it back to level, apologize. "And I was going to tell you about the ghosts."

"Is that why you didn't want to go to your house?"

"No, it's because…" he hesitated. "Maybe.

They pop up there a lot. There are a lot of places, my people lived all over town, married into other families…" He stopped. He was babbling. "Adele."

"I know," she said, holding up a hand to stop him. He could see that she was shivering. "It's not that. It's that you didn't tell me. I think you should go. For now."

"For now?" He grasped at the straw of hope.

"Look, Dan," she said, and he hated that she'd crossed her arms over her chest, backing away from him. With the long knife still clutched in her hand, she waved toward where the specter had been. The chill of the ghost's presence lingered in the room. "This isn't in my wheelhouse."

"I've lived in Haven Harbor all my life," he said, knowing he had one shot. He couldn't blow it. "Most of my friends don't know about this," he waved at the air of the kitchen. "Only Pere, Sam and Jake know. I was going to tell you when we were talking the other night. I was going to tell you. Let you decide if you were okay with it."

She nodded. "I get that. I do. I just need you to go now. I need to think about it."

She hadn't shut the door. Not all the way.

"Will you let me come back?"

She gripped her arms tighter around her midsection. It evidently made her realize that she still wore his shirt. She unbuttoned it, and with pride and grace handed it to him.

"Here. I'm going to go get dressed."

"Can we talk about this? Please?"

She turned at the kitchen door, a goddess clothed only in warm skin and tousled hair. "Maybe. I don't know right now. Are there other things? Other secrets?"

He didn't hesitate. "Yes. I worked for the FBI. I left because of *them*, the ghosts. I got my library degree. I worked in New York. In St. Louis. The job here came open and I came home."

"That it?"

"I'm rich."

She almost smiled. "Good to know."

"What about you?" he said, grasping at straws. "Do you have secrets you haven't told me about?"

He watched her carefully. When her expression closed, he knew he'd hit the mark.

"What? Adele? What are you hiding?"

"Nothing supernatural," she said, crossing her arms again as she stopped in the doorway. She looked sad, and determined. "I was kidnapped, but not like Gabrielle. I was an adult. It was in Mexico seven years ago." She shifted to show him the scar on her side. "The police rescued us, but in the fight, the kidnappers killed my husband."

Horrified at what she'd been through, at the fact she was having to relive it with Hatter and Gabrielle's situation, he started to move forward. She stopped him with a harsh laugh and a turned back. "Yeah, I sometimes feel like a black widow when I tell people. Especially men. You're better off knowing. And leaving."

She walked out of the room. The dogs stared at him. Hatter had finally stopped growling. The dog got up, got a drink and came back to stare at him.

His suit coat, shoes, socks and belt thudded to the floor at the base of the stairs.

CHAPTER SEVEN

The owls came back after he left.

Adele waited until she heard him drive away to go back downstairs. She and the dogs went out the back door, and there were the owls. She nearly cried then, because her first thought—despite everything that had happened—was to call Dan so he could see them.

It only took a few minutes to remove the bandage on the big owl's foot and put more antibiotics on the bird's injury. When the owl and his companions had flown off again, she couldn't make herself go back inside. She didn't want to go to bed, not in the rumpled sheets that smelled of Dan and would now be forever marked by his presence.

Instead, she slept on the couch. Work

dragged the next day. There was no word from Suarez when she sent the info about the bats. Jake returned the text she sent him, but only to say he didn't know anything, but something was happening because Emerson had warned him off.

She walked through town at lunch time, trying to cheer herself up with the amazing Halloween décor that graced virtually every store, light post and flat surface in the town. Lydia's giant broom in front of The Besom Shop was twined with orange lights that winked on and off. A good dozen carved pumpkins sat on hay bales, surrounded by mums. More brooms, and carved Jack-o-Lanterns on the hay bales, brightened the front entrance. The Enchanted Florist was even more impressive with golden leaves, amazing flowers and more pumpkins. Every shop, large and small had an amazing Halloween display.

Darlene and the techs had decorated the clinic too, but in a more subdued fashion—nothing noisy, and no props with sudden movements or voices. They didn't want anyone's pet to be inadvertently spooked, but they'd used lots of mums, gourds and pumpkins of all shapes and sizes.

She admired the white gourds as she

returned to the clinic.

Dan hadn't contacted her, nor she him. Even if he had, what would she say?

"You okay, honey?" Darlene said as she was about to lock up that evening. "You look a little down. You and your hunky guy have a falling out?"

Adele frowned. "Yes. Sort of. He had a couple of important things going on that he surprised me with. I wasn't sure what to do about them," Adele said, keeping it vague. "I had a couple of things I hadn't told him either. Like that I'd been married before. Widowed," she added when Darlene looked shocked.

"Well, I didn't know that either. Huh." Darlene looked surprised. "The things you learn. Well? Did you talk it out?"

"No, I needed a little space to process things."

"That's smart," Darlene said with a sharp nod. "But don't leave it too long, you hear? You wouldn't want to lose such a good man over something small, right? Just ask yourself how big and important whatever it is, in the scheme of things." She patted Adele on the shoulder and said, "Good night now."

Adele stood in the empty clinic for a few more minutes, thinking. She drove home, still pondering the situation. "What's so wrong with a little space?" she said, hearing the whine in her own voice, and hated it.

When she got home, she put on boots and walked the property under the light of a waxing crescent moon. The dogs walked with her. When they got to the back fence, barely visible in the glow from her rear-garden spotlights, Hatter stood up on the bars of the six-foot fence sniffing the air. He whined, and dropped down to all fours, pacing along the fence line.

When she called to him, he came, reluctantly. When she turned to go toward the house, Hatter kept running back to the fence, whining.

Watching him, she remembered that Dan's grandfather's ghost had said something about the dog.

"What was it? What did he say?" She looked to the dogs. Dammit, what had he said. The dogs didn't answer. "C'mon Hatter."

She looked at Hercules and Patronus and thought about the previous night. "Some help you were, Patronus, hiding behind me when Grampa's scary ghost showed up."

The dog looked at her, whined and ducked his head. "Don't worry, darling boy," she said, laughing as she rubbed his head. "I was pretty freaked out too."

Yeah, freaked out, didn't you Adele? First sign of trouble, you duck and run.

An ex-boyfriend had said that. He'd said a lot of other things too. Some of them mean, but some of them true. Dan was right as well, she'd kept some secrets.

She'd also freaked out at the first sign of trouble. The first sign of a *difference*.

He hadn't.

He hadn't batted an eye when she'd worked on the owl. She could tell he'd wanted to jerk her back, out of harm's way. Just like he'd wanted to do at the clinic. He'd apologized for that. He'd been right behind her when she'd been stupid enough to go charging in with just a bat.

Adele might have yelled at him too, if the positions had been reversed.

And she'd thrown him out for talking to ghosts.

"Not like it was another woman," she said, her voice echoing in the October night. As she stood there, her decorations lit up. She had everything on a timer, so all the purple and orange lights that ran along the front fence winked on. In virtually every window, a candle or pumpkin glowed. She knew that, inside the house, various lighted props had turned on as well.

She put a foot on the back step to go in, but Hatter whined and ran to the car. He ran back to her, then back to the car.

"What?"

She knelt as the dog came back. He sat in front of her, whining and making a growly-moaning sort of sound. She took a deep breath and concentrated, trying to *see* what the dog was trying to tell her.

Flashes of the girl she'd seen before. A frantic whine from Hatter as he ran to the car. When she didn't move, he ran all the way to the back fence. She could hear him barking in the distance.

Everything clicked into place.

"He can smell her. Somehow he can smell her on the wind."

Adele was driving slowly down the road, with Hatter hanging half out of the window. If he whined, she turned or slowed. When he didn't do anything else, she kept going. It was like playing Marco Polo without any edge to the pool.

When lights shone on the road behind her, she pulled to the shoulder to let whoever it was pass.

She recognized the SUV. It pulled up next to her, and the passenger side window rolled down. Dan was in the passenger seat, and his friend, Sam Samuels, was driving.

"Adele, the ghosts said you needed help."

She sat for a minute, staring at him. "And you came."

"Of course."

Of course. Just like that. He backed her up even when she'd told him to leave. How many times had he done that for people? How many times had he been rejected?

"I called Jake," she said after greeting Sam. "He's in Pennyfield at a meeting. Suarez is in Boston. I don't know how to contact Emerson."

"I'm glad you texted me as well. We better figure out what Hatter knows so we can have something to show them when they get back."

"I think it's the Gilman place," she said. "The one with the bats."

"Why did you think there was something off?"

"I'm not sure. There was no one there when I went by, but Darlene said she'd seen someone there. She stopped, being neighborly. The guy said he was a handyman, working on the house. She didn't think much of it. It doesn't seem right to me, though. It nagged at me, but I figured it out. There's no work going on in that house. Workmen leave tools, have cars. Darlene said there was no car or truck."

"Yeah, that's off all right. No one should be there," Sam spoke for the first time. "I own that old place."

"You do?" Dan and Adele said it at the same time.

Sam grinned. "Yeah. I'm going to fix it up at some point. When I can."

"Idiot," Dan punched him in the arm, then turned back to Adele. "We won't have to worry about trespassing then."

By mutual agreement, they drove till they were just shy of the Gilman place. They parked along the shoulder, turning off their lights.

Adele got Hatter out of the car. She'd put him on a leash, but she wasn't sure she could control him if he scented Gabrielle.

The three of them ducked up the driveway, and into the apple trees that lined the left side. The fallen apples crunched under their boots and Hatter strained into the collar. His whine so soft as to be sub-vocal at this point, but she could feel the vibration of it along the lead.

"Let's take it slow," Dan said, and she saw Sam grin. Somehow, she doubted this was the first time the two men had gone sneaking around at night.

Slow would have been good, but Hatter pulled hard toward the driveway even as she tried to keep them in the trees. They hadn't gone twenty feet when she felt a chill wind, just like she had in her kitchen.

"Dan," she hissed, pulling on his jacket. First she pointed at Hatter, handing him the leash. Adele was strong, but Hatter was leaning into the collar so steadily, he was about to pull her off her feet. Then she pointed behind her. "It's getting cold again."

The cold intensified, and Dan pivoted, as did Sam.

"Great. Not now," he said in a harsh whisper. Sam rolled his eyes and Dan explained. "I know, but if one of my ancestors lived here, there's probably a family ghost here. If I set foot on a family property, they'll come eventually. Since I'm related to most of the old families in the county, I get visitors." He let the words trail away as the ghost took form.

Turning to it he started to speak, to order it to go.

"Wait," Adele said, her hand squeezing his

arm. "If it knows the house, can it go in and see if the little girl is there?"

Dan stared at her as if she'd lost her mind, but then, he smiled. Bending low, he kissed her cheek. "You're brilliant."

"I know," she said in jest, smiling back.

"Daniel Joseph Baines Nutter! Did you just kiss that young woman?" a prissy voice slid into the darkness. The ghost formed into a vaguely female shape, her hands on her hips. "And in the orchard this late at night? I'm shocked, I tell you. You'll have to speak to her father right away. You can't have a woman's reputation ruined, being out with a man this late!"

"Auntie Agatha?" he asked.

"Heavens no, boy. Do I look like that dried up old spinster? It's your Great-Great Grandmother Howell. Now, what are you going to do to protect that young woman's virtue, I ask you?"

"I'll talk to her father, Grandmother Howell. In the morning. In the meantime, could you tell me who's in the house?"

The ghost didn't answer him, just peered at Adele and Sam. "Oh, that's the dog Frederick was talking about. The young lady in the house owns the dog, I believe."

"That's what the ghost in the kitchen said,"

Adele interrupted, reminding Dan of the encounter. "To look to the dog for answers. That's why I was out on the road."

"So the little girl's in the house?" Dan demanded.

"Yes, she is. Quite a fetching creature," Agatha said. "She plays an impressive game of chess."

"What is it saying?" Sam asked. He couldn't see the ghost. Agatha turned to him, and become almost solid. Sam's eyes widened. Evidently he could see her now.

"Oh yes. The young lady can see me. Just like I can make you see me, Sam Samuels. Your father's related to Daniel's mother's people." Agatha smiled. "There must be some of the blood there in that girl, somewhere. Anyway, she beat me two games out of five which is the first time that's happened since…" she trailed off, obviously trying to reckon the years. Eventually, she shrugged. "For a long time."

"Is she okay?" Adele asked, wondering why she could see the ghost, she certainly wasn't related to Dan. "The little girl?"

"Oh, yes," Agatha said, turning to her. "For now. That unpleasant man though, you'll need to deal with him."

"Okay. Great," Dan said to his ancestress.

"Is there just one?"

"Yes, although another one is due back soon."

"Shit, the cars!" Sam said. "They're right there where anyone coming in can see them."

"We've got to move them."

"We need to wait for Jake," Adele said. She'd almost screwed this up before, at the clinic, and she wasn't going to chance Gabrielle's safety or Dan's for that matter. Despite what had happened to her, they had to wait for the law.

"Right," Dan said, looking toward the house. It appeared to be dark and abandoned unless you knew what to look for. There was the faintest sliver of light around the edge of several of the boarded up windows. Upstairs, there was light as well, but it was even fainter than the downstairs.

There was a brush of wind and an updraft as an owl flew through the next row of trees, rising to sit on the roof peak.

"Oh!" Adele said, watching as several more lighted on the roof as well.

"We'll let the bird keep watch," Dan said, and Sam just shrugged.

"It's a Haven Harbor kind of night," Sam said as they headed for the road. "Let's get out of here and wait for the cavalry. I'll text

Jake and let him know we found the girl."

"Don't you forget to make this right, Daniel," Agatha hissed. "You don't get to dally with women's affections and leave them hanging you know. No grandson of mine—"

"Don't worry, Grandmother Agatha," Adele said. "I'll make sure he does the right thing."

Dan shot her a grin as he tugged Hatter's leash. Dan was strong enough to pull Hatter back with them as they moved through the trees. With his back to the house, Sam pulled out his phone to text Jake.

Sam: Found the girl at the Gilman place. The ghosts confirmed. Also, dog alerted.

Jake: We're on our way, full out. Game is up. They caught the leader at the money drop, but he's dead. Suicide by cop. Two others in custody. We very nearly had them all. I'm sending Jim and Chase to you. Wait for them! Bad guys will probably try to kill the girl.

Sam: Tell them to hurry.

"We have to hurry," Sam said. "Jake says they caught the leader trying to pick up money, but the guy's dead. We don't want these guys to catch us here."

They got to the cars, backed them off around the bend. The dark night settled around them.

"What do we do now?" Adele whispered.

"Wait."

The word was barely out of Dan's mouth when a flash of lights turning into the driveway of the old Gilman place made each of them catch their breath.

"That was a near thing," Sam said. They were waiting in Sam's SUV. The dog sat in the back next to Adele, whining and periodically pawing at the door.

"Where are Jim and Chase?" Dan fretted. "They should be here by now."

"I don't know. Something's wrong," Sam said. "What if the bad guys know about their leader getting killed? What if they're going to move her?"

"Or worse," Dan added, hand on the door handle. "We should block the driveway."

Before Sam or Adele could agree, Grandmother Agatha suddenly appeared in the car, her cold presence sending shivers through everyone.

"Boy, you need to come right now. They're dragging that little mite downstair. I think they're going to hurt her."

No sooner were the words spoken, than four owls landed on the hood of the car, then took off again for the house.

"Shit." Sam jumped down from the

driver's seat to the road and began to run.

"Adele, wait," Dan began as she jumped out of the truck as well, Hatter dragging her toward the old house. Dan caught up with her, taking the leash. Together they followed Sam to the end of the drive.

When they stopped, she forestalled anything else Dan was going to say by kissing him. "We'll both be careful. We have a lot to talk about."

CHAPTER EIGHT

They reached the apple trees again, and moved toward the house. Before they'd gone far, they heard the crunch of tires on gravel. The sheriff's cruiser inched into the driveway. The car bore no lights and crept an inch at a time into the property.

"Don't move." Dan's whisper was like a shout in the silence. "If he sees movement in the trees, he might fire."

"Carl?" She couldn't believe the sheriff would even pull a gun, much less fire it. He seemed like a harmless old teddy bear.

"He's trained law enforcement," Dan reminded them. "If he doesn't know we're here, and sees us creeping through the trees, he'll assume we're hostiles."

"That would suck," Sam said, dropping

even lower into the shadows.

Hatter made no sound but he strained and strained at the leash. Adele had taken him back when the sheriff appeared, but it took all her strength to hold him.

Suddenly, there was a light at the door and a man ran out to a black SUV with blacked out windows. That must have been the car they'd hear pulling in. The man tossed two duffels into the back. He was turning back to the house when the sheriff cut on his lights, turned on the spotlight from his driver's side, and the red lights on top of the vehicle. His voice boomed out into the night.

"Stop there, sir. This is the Haven Harbor Sheriff. Put your hands where I can see them—"

There was the boom of gunfire and the cruiser's windshield shattered. The driver's side door opened and Carl Lackner rolled out, to lie flat on the ground, firing at the man who continued to fire at him.

It was the man by the SUV who went down.

"Carl!" Sam called, "Its Sam Samuels, are you hit?"

"Sam? What in the Gods' name are you doing out here? You young idiot, you coulda been shot."

"Are you hit?" Sam called, ignoring the reprimand.

"Yeah," Carl cursed. "Right above the body armor, and in the thigh."

"I'm coming to you," Sam dashed toward the vehicle, leaving Adele and Dan with the dog. The moment's distraction, as Sam ran, was enough for Hatter to tug his leash free and bound toward the house.

"Crap! The dog!" Adele said, racing after him.

Dan followed her. "Adele!" He was fast, but she was faster. They pelted through the trees, and he shouted, "Agatha, you better be here to help!" just as Hatter hit the door and ran in.

Within seconds there was a scream from inside the house.

A man ran outside with Hatter snarling at his heels. From the roof peak, three owls swooped down to batter at the man's head. The man fired wildly into the air, missing the owls, and enraging the dog.

A young girl, dressed in ill-fitting jeans and a pink top ran onto the porch. "Hatter, to me," she yelled, and the dog backed off, blocking her and pushing her backwards into the house.

"Dan!" Adele screamed as the fallen man

rolled to his side and trained the gun on the dog and the girl.

"Agatha!" he shouted, and a bright mist coalesced in front of the man. As the mist lowered, the man screamed. Dan raced forward, jumping onto the porch and kicking the gun away, just like she'd seen on television. The man was still screaming as Dan flipped him over and yanked his hands up behind his back.

"Here, Carl said you'd need these." Sam tossed him the cuffs before dashing off to the black SUV to check on the second gunman.

Adele had run for Hatter and Gabrielle the moment it looked like Dan had the situation under control.

Hatter had backed Gabrielle into a corner, and he blocked her in, facing outward. He was growling like a Hellhound.

Adele stopped, projecting calm. "Are you Gabrielle?" she asked, squatting down to be at the girl's level. "And this is your dog, Hatter."

"Yes. I'm Gabrielle Spradling. My dad is Thomas Spradling. Can you help me?"

"I'm Dr. Adele Picard. I took care of Hatter when those horrible people dumped him. I met your dad. He's very nice."

The girl still looked suspicious, until a moment later when Adele felt the chill of

Agatha's presence.

"It's all right, young lady. She's one of the good ones," the ghost said, laying her hand on Adele's shoulder. The feeling was like being dunked in an icebound pond without warning, and Adele gasped. "Oh, beg your pardon," the ghost said, lifting her hand. She spoke to the girl. "Has anyone called your daddy yet? If not, they should. He'll be frantic."

"No ma'am, we haven't hand a chance," Adele answered.

"See that my grandson does that right soon now," she said. Smiling at Gabrielle, she said, "don't worry, youngling. I'll come find you for a rematch sometime."

"Thank you Mrs. Agatha," the girl said, still gripping Hatter's collar. "I'll be glad to see you."

An owl swooped in the door, settling on a tall, dust-and-cobweb-covered lamp. Adele turned to it and it was all she could do not to roll her eyes. Everyone was checking in.

"Thank you for your help," she said, bowing toward the owl. It seemed to be the thing to do. The owl clicked its beak, raised one taloned foot, and then swept back out of the room on silent wings.

"Wow," Gabrielle said, staring after the bird. "That was an owl." She looked at

Adele, her eyes wide. "He bowed to you. That's amazing."

"More amazing than playing chess with a ghost?"

Gabrielle laughed, and the sound was high and happy. A child's unfettered delight. "She's the first ghost I ever met. She was nice."

"Adele!" Dan hurried in the door, grabbed her and crushed her in his arms. "Are you okay?" He pulled away, patting her arms, and her back. "Not hurt?"

"I'm fine. Dan, this is Miss Gabrielle Spradling." She turned to Gabrielle. "This is Mr. Nutter, he's the town librarian."

"Really? I love the library," the little girl said, staring at Dan. "You don't look like a librarian."

Adele laughed. "I said the same thing."

"Is he your boyfriend?" Gabrielle asked, looking tired now, and leaning on the massive dog. The dog had calmed, and leaned right back.

Adele turned to Dan. "I don't know. Are you my boyfriend, Dan Nutter?"

There was a breath of cold air and a soft voice said, "Don't disappoint me, grandson."

"Jeez, of all the times to interfere," Dan muttered. To Gabrielle, he said, "I'd like to be her boyfriend, but I hurt her feelings a little while ago. I was going to ask her if she'd forgive me."

The little girl's gaze swiveled to Adele. "I'm sorry he hurt your feelings," she said simply. "Will you forgive him?"

"Yes, I was planning on it."

"Oh, good," Gabrielle said, sitting down on the floor so she could better lean on Hatter. "Before my mom went to heaven, she used to say that you should never go to bed mad at people you love." To Dan, she said, "You should kiss her now."

"Okay," Dan said, and turned to Adele. "I'm sorry I hurt your feelings. I promise never to keep secrets from you."

"I forgive you, Dan Nutter. I promise the same. So, I've got a few to share with you."

"More owls?"

"Something like that," Adele said. "Some family skeletons."

Dan's eyes widened. "Ghosts?" he murmured, too low for the little girl to hear.

"Ah, no," Adele said, wishing she could evade. "Politicians."

"Oh, my," Dan said, but there was a twinkle in his eye. He bent to kiss her. "I'll forgive you anything, even politicians."

"Okay." She kissed him back. "I'll give

you my father's number so Agatha's satisfied," she teased. He'll be in DC, since Congress is back in session."

Dan pulled back. "Seriously?"

She nodded.

"Okay, then. Hey Gabrielle," he said, turning to the girl. "How about we get you out of here? Your dad is on his way. Did you know that Hatter's been staying with Dr. Adele's for the last few days?"

Gabrielle smiled at his words. She straightened, and when Dan moved in to pick her up, she let him. She laid her head on his shoulder and he cradled her in his arms. Hatter stuck close to Dan's side as they moved across to the door.

"Close your eyes for a minute, honey," Dan said, shielding her from the view of the other kidnapper's body. The second man still lay cuffed on the porch, moaning about the cold and the things that moved in the dark.

As they reached the sheriff's cruiser, Adele heard sirens. Within minutes, Jake had pulled into the driveway in his Bronco, lights flashing. Right behind him were two black sedans with blue lights stuck on their roofs. The second one hadn't even stopped, before a man jumped out it. He raced up the driveway.

"Gabrielle!"

"Daddy!"

The dog barked as Thomas Spradling reached them. Gabrielle jumped from Dan's arms to her father's, and Thomas Spradling, his face streaked with tears, gripped his daughter's slim form as if he would never let her go. Hatter moved to sit on his feet, scanning the darkness for threats.

"Adele," Dan said quietly, pulling her into an embrace. "I'm really sorry."

"Me too."

She turned to survey the scene. Sam knelt by the cruiser, but an ambulance pulled up and he shouted orders for the EMTs to hustle. He tossed Dan his keys as they lifted Carl Lackner onto a backboard and ran him to the ambulance, Sam in tow.

"Guess we'll be driving his car back for him," Dan said, as the ambulance executed a three-point turn in the road and roared toward Haven Harbor's regional medical center.

"He can pick it up at my house."

Dan looked down at her. "You're sure?"

She nodded. "Sometimes, I'm an idiot. Having a ghost appear in my kitchen is a first for me."

"It's not normal, that's for sure," he said

153

with a wry twist to his lips. "I never know where they're going to pop up."

"Do you see ghosts everywhere?" She'd wondered about that.

"No, and newer buildings are great. None of my people's ghosts there."

"You only see your ancestors?"

"Yeah. But not my parents. Grands, and older. A couple of great-aunts or uncles. But only family. And not a single one interested in crossing over or moving on."

"Is it a curse?"

He looked down at her. "I don't think so, despite Grandpa's wailing. I think the ones who want to go on do, and the ones that want to stay, stay."

Jake strode up the drive, checking the body by the SUV before turning their way.

"Adele?" Dan said, wishing Jake would take just a little longer to get to them.

"Hmm?" she replied, enjoying the heat of him as they stood in the chilly night.

"Will you go to the Halloween Ball with me?"

She laughed. "You ask now? In the middle of all of this?"

"Yeah."

She poked at him, her finger meeting firm muscle.

"Of course I'll go with you." She wanted his body next to hers, with her, in bed. Now. "When can we go home?"

"Soon," he said, and when she looked up, he was smiling down at her.

"You two," Jake called, "are in trouble."

EPILOGUE

"Ready?" Dan said as she opened the door. Then he just gaped. She was the most gorgeous thing he'd ever seen. "Wow, you look amazing."

She blushed and mock-curtseyed. "Why thank you, kind sir."

The late October wind whistled through the bare trees and he added, "You better get a coat."

She pushed open the door in invitation, but he shook his head. "If I come in, we might not leave."

"And that's a bad thing, why?" Adele asked, picking up her coat and evening bag.

"It isn't but I want to show off. I want everyone to see that the most beautiful woman in Haven Harbor is on my arm."

Adele laughed and shooed the dogs back into the house when they would have surged out to greet Dan. "Hatter's at the hotel. Gabrielle wants us to sneak up with her sometime tonight, or come by tomorrow to see him."

"I'm glad we invited her and Thomas to come to the Ball." Dan offered his arm, walking with her down the steps.

"I am too," Adele agreed. "I think you and he need to have a chat about Gabrielle and the ghosts."

"Gabrielle and the Ghosts," he chuckled over the words. "Sounds like a b-grade movie title."

She laughed and he handed her into the car. When he handed her out again at the Inn, tossing his keys to the teenage valet he recognized from the high school, he felt like the luckiest man alive.

"This is so exciting," she said, eyes shining. "I've only been to one other Ball and I came stag."

"I remember," he said and she gave him a surprised look. "It was your second year in town, I'd just come back. You'd just joined the civic club and the Coven the same year."

"Oh. You're in both, right?"

"Yep. That first Coven meeting you came

to, I nearly swallowed my tongue when I saw you."

She shot him a smile. "I wish you'd have made a move."

"Me too. I'm glad I finally did it now."

They laughed as they passed their coats to yet another teen managing a coat check. They were directed into a corner that held a display of pumpkins, mums and sheaves of corn for a photo.

"I plan to pull you into dark corners all night, and kiss you to be sure you remember who you came with," Dan whispered

She laughed and wiggled her eyebrows. "As long as you remember who you came with too," she said saucily.

He mock-growled at her. "Mind your manners wench," he replied in the same teasing vein. "Or I might kiss you again."

"Oh, please do," she added, still laughing.

They entered the main ballroom to the sound of bouncy dance music. The swing band was getting the crowd warmed up, with couples already on the dance floor. Others were in buffet lines, and more were clustered at tables all around the room, chatting.

Later they'd go from the ball to the Coven circle, to celebrate Samhain, but until then, he was going to dance with Adele.

He pulled her toward the dance floor. "Dance with me."

Adele admired the decorations as she and Dan moved in one another's arms, swaying to the music. The general theme of the décor was vintage Halloween, with festive fall touches. The lighted panels and moons were lovely and Adele decided that next year, she was getting on the decorating committee.

They danced on and off all throughout the evening. Now, as midnight approached Dan danced with Gabrielle in his arms, and Adele took a turn around the dance floor with Thomas Spradling.

"I know I thanked you already," Thomas said as they stopped dancing to watch Dan and Gabrielle. Thomas's features looked less gaunt in the light of the dangling moons and stars that dripped from the ceiling.

"Gabrielle's a sweet girl and doesn't seem to have suffered too much." Adele put a comforting hand on his arm.

"She's resilient," he agreed. "To her, being home and having Hatter back is all that matters. That happened, thanks to you," Thomas said, his eyes never leaving his little girl. Adele didn't know what to say to that, so they stood in companionable silence for a few moments.

"I'm thinking of moving to Haven Harbor," Thomas said suddenly. "Gabrielle says she wants to go to school where your Dan is the librarian." He turned to her and smiled. "I think she's got a crush."

Watching Dan with the little girl as they laughed their way around the dance floor, Adele felt her heart melt. "She'll have to get in line, because I've got a crush on him too," she said.

Thomas laughed. "I know."

Noting the time, Dan whirled Gabrielle into a dip, then picked her up and delivered her to Thomas. "You daughter, good sir!"

"Why thank you, Mr. Nutter," Thomas pretended to be formal as well, bowing slightly. "Job well done. And now, my lady Gabrielle," her father said, "It's nearly midnight. We should be heading out before you and I turn into pumpkins!"

"That never happens in Haven Harbor," Dan quipped, but his eyes were on Adele. He held out his hand. He had a midnight promise to keep. The Coven had work soon, but for now, he had a very personal appointment. "A dance, milady?"

"Anytime." She let him lead her onto the dance floor. She didn't notice other people leaving the dance floor until it was totally empty. Lucille Birkland was on the dais with the band, waiting to lead them to the Coven circle. For now, however, since she knew his plan, she was beaming at them.

"Dan?" Adele lifted her head from his shoulder, looking around at the people who stood, watching them.

The music dropped in volume and Dan stopped their swaying progress, and dropped to one knee. "Adele, I talked to your father," he said softly, the words meant only for the two of them. "He gave me his permission to ask you."

Eyes wide, she stared at him. "You talked to my dad?" Shock was written on her face, and she was vaguely aware of tittering laughs from the crowd when her words rang out into the quiet. You could have heard a pin drop in the brightly decorated ballroom.

"I did. And your mom. But the most important person I want to talk to is right in front of me. Dr. Adele Picard, will you marry me?"

To his delight, she positively gaped at the enormous diamond solitaire he presented her. He'd noticed that she wore mostly silver or platinum, so that's what he'd picked for the ring.

"Yes," she said, bending down to kiss him while the room exploded in applause. She rested her brow against his. "I love you, Dan Nutter, ghosts and all."

"I love you Adele Picard, dogs, attack cats, politicians and all."

She laughed and he picked her up and swung her around to the cheers and applause of all.

"Witches of Haven Harbor," Lucille Birkland called cheerfully into the microphone. "It's time!"

"You're my Halloween promise, Adele," he said, taking her mouth in a long, hot kiss as he stopped twirling her around. "Always."

She framed his face with her hands, drawing him down into another lush kiss. "Always, my love. Always."

ABOUT JEANNE ADAMS

Jeanne Adams likes calling North Carolina home, but for now, she lives in DC, with her husband, two sons, and three dogs. Jeanne's favorite holiday is Halloween and she starts planning the annual yard decor for each year as soon as the current Halloween is over. As an amateur genealogist, Jeanne was researching her husband's Adams relatives and discovered one had been accused in the Witch Trials in Salem. (He escaped...) Thus was the genesis of The Witches Walk.

On another spooky and suspenseful note, Jeanne used to work in the funeral and cemetery business, and knows a thing or two about getting rid of the body....bwhahahah! (She even teaches classes about it for writers!) She claims that's one reason she took up writing romantic suspense! Jeanne has written award-winning suspense novels for Kensington/Zebra Publishing since 2007, including the highly acclaimed DEADLY LITTLE SECRETS, and its follow up, DEADLY LITTLE LIES. An excerpt from DEADLY LITTLE SECRETS was featured in Cosmopolitan Magazine.

For updates on all Jeanne's work, check her website - www.JeanneAdams.com where you can sign up for her newsletter.
Follow her on Twitter @JeanneAdams
Follow her on Facebook at
www.Facebook.com/JeanneAdamsAuthor.

TITLES BY JEANNE ADAMS

SUSPENSE
DEAD RUN, Faithful Defenders #1
DEADLY DELIVERY (Novella)
CAPITOL DANGER (With Suzanne Ferrell, JD Tyler,
and Nancy Northcott)

HISTORICAL
BEHIND ENEMY LINES (WWII)

URBAN FANTASY
THE TENTACLE AFFAIRE

HAVEN HARBOR SERIES
WITCHES WALK
A MIDNIGHT PROMISE, Novella in WELCOME TO
HAVEN HARBOR (Haven Harbor 1.25)

FORTHCOMING BOOKS
A YULE TO REMEMBER, Novella in UNDER THE
KISSING BOUGH (Haven Harbor 1.50), November
2016
A SPIRITED LIFE, A Green Magic Novel, January 2017
THE RUM RUNNER INCIDENT, Slip Traveler #2,
March 2017

TITLES CAN BE FOUND AT ALL MAJOR
RETAILERS

Made in the USA
Middletown, DE
14 October 2017